## It was a strange sensation.

The feel of Webb's hand was doing strange things to Bonnie. She let her hand lie in his as he opened the gate and ushered her through, anxious not to appear ungracious by pulling it away. . .

Anxious not to pull away. . .

She had a feeling of being cared for—a feeling as novel as it was extraordinary. The warmth from his hand crept through her entire body and she ventured a look up at him. To her confusion he was looking down at her, his eyes filled with the laughter she'd always suspected they could contain.

**Marion Lennox** has had a variety of careers—medical receptionist, computer programmer and teacher. Married, with two young children, she now lives in rural Victoria, Australia. Her wish for an occupation which would allow her to remain at home with her children and her dog led her to begin writing, and she has now published a number of medical romances.

**Recent titles by the same author:**

ENCHANTING SURGEON
DANGEROUS PHYSICIAN
DOCTOR'S HONOUR
PRACTICE MAKES MARRIAGE
STORM HAVEN
ONE CARING HEART

# A CHRISTMAS BLESSING

BY

MARION LENNOX

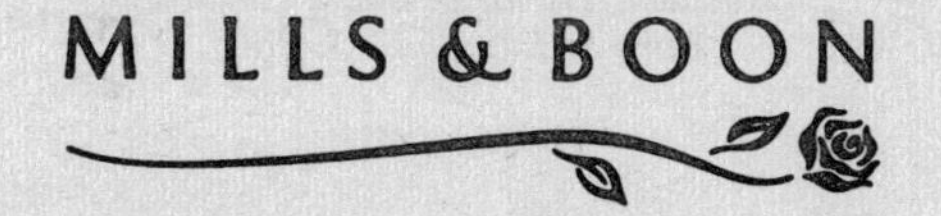

*All the characters in this book have no existence outside the imagination of the author, and have no relation whatsoever to anyone bearing the same name or names. They are not even distantly inspired by any individual known or unknown to the author, and all the incidents are pure invention.*


*Harlequin Mills & Boon Limited,*
*Eton House, 18-24 Paradise Road, Richmond, Surrey TW9 1SR*
*This edition published by arrangement with Harlequin Enterprises B.V.*



ISBN 0 263 79404 0

*Set in Times 10 on 11 pt. by*
*Rowland Phototypesetting Limited*
*Bury St Edmunds, Suffolk*

*03-9512-48432*

*Made and printed in Great Britain*
*Cover illustration by Anthony Meadows*

## CHAPTER ONE

'PHONE for you, Dr Gaize. A Dr Webb Halford.'

Webb Halford. . . Dr Bonnie Gaize ran her hand through her short curls in a gesture of fatigue. 'Who on earth is Dr Halford? He isn't a staff member.'

'He must be a new consultant.' The charge nurse grimaced expressively. 'He sounds dictatorial enough to be really important.'

A consultant. An overbearing consultant throwing his weight around was the last thing she needed now. Bonnie had one more patient to see and then she was on holiday.

'Could you tell Dr Halford I'm off duty and unavailable as of ten minutes ago? Luke Mitchim's taken over from me. Put him through to Luke.'

On holiday. . .

The recorded Christmas music echoed through the ward as Bonnie pulled the screens around her favourite patient.

'I've been singing that song "White Christmas" in my head for the last six months,' she confessed. 'Ten days to Christmas—and then I'll be making snowballs instead of sweltering in Melbourne's heat.'

'Snow's over-rated.' The gaunt-faced Irishman lay back on his pillows and refused to be impressed. 'Why do you think I migrated all the way to Australia?'

'Because you wanted to see the world, just like me.' Bonnie lifted a wrist as she talked, noting the lack of flesh on his arm with concern. 'Paddy, are you still not eating?' She looked down at his untouched plate of dinner.

'No. I don't feel like it, girl, and why should I force down what I don't want?'

Bonnie nodded. It was Paddy's choice not to eat, and she could understand his reasons. Emphysema combined with financial troubles had forced Paddy off his farm and a car accident had smashed his leg. During two months of traction, Paddy's emphysema had worsened to the stage where he couldn't go home but it didn't matter—he had no home to go to.

Paddy pushed the food away with disgust. 'It smells of antiseptic,' he growled. 'Like everything else in this place. What I'd give to get a decent whiff of cow dung again—and there's not a lot of that in the nursing home they're threatening me with. And now. . . Now even you're deserting me, girl.'

Bonnie replaced the Irishman's bony wrist on the coverlet as she perched on the edge of the bed. The charge nurse hated doctors sitting on beds, but then, Paddy was her last patient for the day. . .

Paddy was her last patient for months. Now was the beginning of Bonnie's first ever holiday and it was the holiday that dreams were made of. A white Christmas!

'And it's excited you are at the thought of leaving,' Paddy accused.

Bonnie winced. Impulsively she leaned over to give him a swift hug.

'You're my one regret,' she confessed. 'They told me at medical school not to become attached to patients—and why I've attached myself to a recalcitrant old scoundrel like you I don't know!'

'It's my debonair, man-about-town attitude. Plus my red hair.' Paddy attempted a hoot of laughter and then subsided into a fit of coughing. By the time he recovered, Bonnie's smile had slipped. The man's breathing was so tenuous. . .

'I do hate leaving you,' she admitted. 'It's just. . .'

'It's just you've never had a proper holiday, you've finished your internship and you're free for the first time in your life.' Paddy reached forward to grip Bonnie's hand. 'You don't have to tell me, girl. You're the hardest working young doctor round here by a country mile, and my spies tell me you put yourself through medical school. Study by day and waitressing by night. Well, you deserve your holiday. I just wish. . .I just wish I could be alive to hear about it when you get back.'

Silence. Given Paddy's deteriorating condition, there were no promises to be made and both of them knew it. Bonnie let her hand lie in Paddy's and she felt her heart wrench. If only he had a few visitors, or even one. . .

'Get away with you, girl,' the Irishman growled, sensing her thoughts. 'You're no kin of mine and you've a holiday of a lifetime to look forward to. Send me a postcard and be done with it.'

To do anything else was stupid. There would always be patients she was fond of. There would always be a reason not to go—a Paddy.

'Thank you, Paddy,' she whispered and leaned forward to kiss the sunken cheek. Paddy responded by reaching forward to pull her slight body into his arms. To his delight, Dr Gaize let him do it. He ruffled her soft, brown curls with pleasure.

'If I were thirty years younger. . .' he growled. 'You should be wanting to stay home because of a handsome young scoundrel, not because of a wreck like me.'

Bonnie smiled and shook her head as she released herself from his frail hold. She had no illusions as to her ability to attract men, even if Paddy disagreed.

Bonnie is the mousey one. . .

She could still hear echoes of her aunt's voice after

all these years, swiftly pointing out to visitors that the striking child with the huge blue eyes, the svelte figure and the pouting lips was her own adored Jacinta, and Bonnie—tiny Bonnie with brown, nondescript hair, eyes that were as green as Jacinta's were blue and a nose that was distinctly snub, as well as freckled—had been adopted by aunt and uncle after her own parents were killed.

'There's nothing wrong with our Bonnie,' Uncle Henry always retorted, but aunt and cousin had looked pityingly on Bonnie and known better.

Only once had Bonnie ever considered herself pretty. Once, aged twenty-two when she had accepted her first and only proposal of marriage. . .

The evening gowns and frivolous clothes Craig encouraged her to buy had been given to charity long since. Bonnie wore sensible, serviceable clothes, and she would for the rest of her life. Craig had told her she was beautiful, but Craig had lied. . .

She had to stop this. Bonnie gave herself an angry mental shake. There was no pleasure in memories and there was packing to do.

As if in answer to the thought, the curtains around the bed parted and the charge nurse put her head in.

'Dr Gaize, Dr Webb Halford's in Reception to see you,' she told Bonnie. 'He says he's been over to the residence to find you only to be sent back here, and he needs to see you personally—not the doctor on duty. He's in a hurry and it's urgent.' She rolled her eyes at Bonnie and smiled. 'I'd go fast even if it's not urgent,' she twinkled. 'He might sound dictatorial, but wow!' Then her smile slipped and she frowned down at Paddy's bedcover. 'Dr Gaize, have you been sitting on my patients' beds again?'

'I bounced on it meself, Sister,' Paddy retorted and even the stern-voiced charge nurse laughed. Despite her voiced disapproval of Bonnie's bed-sitting, Sister Carter was as fond of Dr Bonnie Gaize as Paddy was.

Bonnie had to go. She didn't have a clue who this Dr Halford was, but there was only one way to find out. She stooped to give Paddy a last, swift kiss.

'Goodbye, Paddy,' she whispered. 'Bless you.'

It was the last time she'd see him. Bonnie turned and walked swiftly out of the ward before Paddy or the nurse could see the sudden tears in her eyes.

Dr Halford. . .

Who on earth was Dr Halford?

Bonnie thought through the doctors she knew as she made her way to Reception. Christmas was the time for staff to be finishing their terms—not starting. Surely she should know the name?

Bonnie racked her brains as she walked swiftly through the hospital, glancing impatiently at her watch as she went. She hadn't had dinner, nor had she started packing. There was so much to do. . .

Whoever Dr Halford was, his business with her had better be fast.

In Reception a stranger stood waiting, his back to the door as he leafed through a magazine. The receptionist gestured towards him, leaving Bonnie in no doubt that this was the man who wanted her.

So who was he? Bonnie frowned as she approached him. The unknown doctor was wearing trousers and a sports coat. Hospital consultants usually wore business suits. This man looked younger than most consultants anyway—in his early thirties at a guess.

Guessing was useless. Bonnie took her hands from the pockets of her white coat and walked forward to touch his shoulder.

'Excuse me. I'm Dr Gaize. I gather you wished to see me.'

Her voice trailed off as the man turned, and Bonnie took an instinctive step back.

Dr Halford was large, but not unusually so—six feet maybe and strongly built. The presence of the man made him seem larger.

Larger? Wrong word, Bonnie thought fleetingly. Stronger maybe. . .

Or maybe just more plain masculine.

With his harsh, accentuated bone structure, piercing eyes set deep in a tanned face and strongly muscled body, this man exuded more masculinity than Bonnie had ever sensed in a single male. His coal black hair heightened the feeling of darkness and strength, and the hand that came forward to grip Bonnie's consolidated her first impressions. Strength. . .

She looked up in faint confusion.

There were laughter lines around the man's penetrating grey eyes, with the suggestion of a twinkle in their depths, but the twinkle was firmly repressed at the moment. Bonnie searched those eyes and felt like a schoolgirl in trouble. In big trouble. . .

'Dr Gaize?' he demanded of her as he shook her hand and then released it. His deep, resonant voice was cold—almost hostile. 'I'm Webb Halford. . .'

'Dr Halford?' Bonnie looked up into those piercing eyes with a sense of misgiving. 'I don't think I know——'

'I'm sure you don't.' It seemed by his voice that she had blundered, but she didn't know how. 'I'm the general practitioner at Kurrara and I'm your father's doctor.'

'My father. . .' Bonnie took a deep breath and closed her eyes in sudden pain. When she opened them the sharp, accustomed ache had receded. 'That's not possible,' she told him, her voice somehow steady. 'My father died when I was ten.'

Silence. The man was looking at her as if he couldn't make up his mind whether she was some sort of nasty piece of insect life or—just maybe—he might have made a mistake. There was a trace of doubt in those all-seeing eyes.

'You are Dr Bonnie Gaize?'

'Yes.'

He nodded. 'And Henry Gaize is your father and Jacinta Gaize is your sister.'

'No.'

The eyes flashed annoyance. 'That's not what they tell me.'

Bonnie met his annoyance head on. She tilted her chin and her clear green eyes didn't flinch.

'Henry Gaize is my uncle,' she said. 'Jacinta is my cousin. I've seen neither for four years.'

'But Henry and your aunt adopted you when your parents died,' Webb Halford said slowly. 'And brought you up as their daughter.'

Bonnie didn't answer. Her eyes fell away. As their daughter. . . That was a joke!

'They did adopt you?' Webb demanded and Bonnie nodded.

'Yes.'

'Did you know your aunt is dead?'

Bonnie's eyes flashed up at him, startled. 'Yes,' she managed. 'I did know that. I. . .I telephoned my uncle when I heard. But. . . But it happened two years ago.'

'And that's the last time you contacted him.'

'Yes.'

'So that was the end of your family obligations?'

Bonnie's green eyes flashed. 'Look, I don't see what business my family relationships are of yours, Dr Halford. If you've something specific to say to me then say it. I'm in a hurry.'

'So I gather,' he said drily. 'Your uncle says you're far too busy to visit him.'

'He doesn't want me to visit him. Now if you'll excuse me. . .'

'If you don't visit him, he'll die.'

As a shock tactic it worked. Bonnie's already pale face drained of remaining colour. She took a step back and stared up at this unknown, accusing doctor.

'What. . . What's wrong with Uncle Henry?'

'Nothing that family couldn't fix.'

'Meaning?' She was getting really angry now. This man was talking in riddles and she didn't like it one bit.

He didn't answer for a moment and she wasn't sure that he would. He stood, looking down at the slip of a girl before him. She hardly looked old enough to be wearing the white coat she had on, yet her name tag established her as a qualified doctor. She looked almost a child. . .

'Your uncle rolled his tractor into a dry creek bed two weeks ago,' Webb Halford said slowly, watching her face. 'He was pinned underneath for almost twenty-four hours before anyone found him. He has a fractured pelvis. . .'

The ties to her family hadn't faded completely. There was still a jab of pain. Bonnie felt her heart sink and she clenched her fists in frustration. She had vowed that it was over, but it seemed—it seemed it wasn't. Would she ever stop caring?

'That's. . . That's all the damage?' she whispered.

'That's all,' Webb said grimly. 'But there's no one to run the farm—your uncle says there's no money to pay someone to milk the cows, let alone a nurse—and it'll be a couple of months before he can look after himself again. By which time the farm will have to be sold. Your uncle has already talked himself into one bout of pneumonia through worry, and he's heading for another. He won't sleep—he just lies and frets. So today—well, I had to come to Melbourne so I thought it wouldn't hurt to come and try and shake a bit of conscience into his adopted daughter.'

'Thanks very much,' Bonnie whispered bleakly. 'Your sense of duty does you credit.'

'More than yours does.' He flashed her a look of intense dislike. The impression that he viewed her as a repellent insect was deepening by the minute. 'Well, I expected nothing less than your reaction. I came to tell you that unless you stirred yourself your uncle would die. That's all. I'll leave you.' And he turned towards the door.

'Just. . . Just a minute.'

It was hardly a command. Bonnie's breath was coming too fast. She was feeling like a small—a very small—animal, caught in a vicious, cutting trap.

'Yes?' He turned cold eyes on her, iced with indifference.

'What. . . What's Jacinta doing in this? She told you about me?'

'I telephoned your cousin in Sydney,' Webb Halford said coldly. 'She has no money to pay for help for your uncle and she has no intention of coming home. She told me your obligation was the greater, and that you were your father's—I mean your uncle's—favourite anyway. It seems to me that he's hardly had much choice.'

Bonnie ignored the slur. 'Jacinta said that?'

'And so did your uncle.' Webb shrugged. 'I asked him about his two daughters. He hardly talked of Jacinta, but he told me all about you—about your career and how well you'd done at medical school. He told me where you were working.'

Bonnie stared up in amazement. 'I didn't think he'd know,' she whispered.

'No. I can believe that.' He looked down at his watch. 'I'm sorry, Dr Gaize but, like you, I'm busy, and I've run out of time. I have to be back in Kurrara tonight. I suppose it's too much to ask that you have some message for your uncle?'

'N. . . No.' Bonnie stared down at her hands. Her mind was twisting in confusion. 'No message.'

'Then I dare say the lawyers will let you know when he dies,' Webb said savagely. 'It'll be soon. And I hope you and your precious sister-cousin inherit exactly what you deserve!'

His scorn lingered for hours.

Bonnie made her way back to her hospital apartment and drearily started packing. The joy had gone right out of it.

London for Christmas.

Bonnie was going to London for Christmas. She was going to shop in Harrods and see the changing of the guard and the Tower of London. She was hiring a car and seeing Oxford and Yorkshire and Wales. . . And then, she was venturing further, to Scotland to search for monsters in Loch Ness and to Paris to climb the Eiffel Tower. . .

She was leaving the traces of her family forever.

'They don't want me,' she told her suitcase. 'They never wanted me. They were saddled with me and they did their duty and then they hurt me so badly. . .so badly that I owe them nothing.

'Not Uncle Henry.

'Uncle Henry stood back and did nothing while Aunt Lois and Jacinta did their worst.

'Uncle Henry loved me. . . Uncle Henry loves me. . .'

The bleak little voice whispered a child's desperate hope into the stillness of her room. A memory came back of Bonnie as a lonely, bereft ten-year-old, screeched at for some misdemeanour by her aunt and finding refuge in the dairy. And Uncle Henry, as always, saying nothing—just putting her on a stool and teaching her to milk. There, in the cold, washed dairy with her uncle watching out of the corner of his eye, she had found some measure of peace.

The pleasure of being with Uncle Henry. . . The pleasure of imagining herself loved. . .

'Without him I would have gone mad,' she told her suitcase and finally, finally she let the lid fall on the half-packed clothes.

'I could spend my holiday money on a nurse and a milker,' she whispered—but where did that leave her? She'd have no money and no job for two months.

She was going to lose her holiday regardless.

I can go to London later, she told herself and knew she wouldn't. Once she started specialist training there would be no holidays for years.

So make the most of it, Bonnie Gaize, she told herself. 'Holidays like this aren't for people like you, and you always knew they weren't. So. . .

So go home and nurse him.

He won't want me there. He won't accept my help.

So think of a way that he will, Bonnie told herself harshly. Think, Dr Gaize.

Unbidden, the thought of Webb Halford's face came into her mind and Bonnie stifled an involuntary gasp.

'And you can stop thinking of that man,' she told herself with a voice that only faintly trembled. 'You're a sensible professional, Bonnie Gaize. Act like one!'

She telephoned Kurrara Hospital first thing the next morning and asked to be put through to Dr Halford. Webb Halford, on the other end of the line, sounded curt and preoccupied.

'I'll be there tomorrow to take my uncle home,' Bonnie told him. 'Could you let him know?'

'You'd better wear a name tag when you come,' Webb said bluntly. 'He's hardly likely to recognise you.'

Bonnie's colour mounted. 'I don't need your insults,' she managed through gritted teeth.

'No. And I wish to heaven your uncle didn't need you. It's going to be no easy job looking after him at home, and if you didn't have a medical degree I wouldn't countenance it for a minute. It's not medicine he needs—it's just plain hard work—but I imagine at least your medical degree will tell you what the outcome of negligent nursing will be.'

'I know that.'

'I wonder,' he said curtly. 'The farm is a mess. Neither your cousin nor yourself seem to have been near it for years. Still, even if your presence does no more than make Henry come to terms with the fact he'll have to sell. . .'

'I'll see you tomorrow,' Bonnie hissed and slammed the receiver down on the cradle.

The man was an arrogant toad! Bonnie fumed for half an hour after the telephone call. He'd obviously put Bonnie and Jacinta in the same category—and two more opposite people could hardly exist.

'He doesn't know what I'm doing, coming home to the farm,' Bonnie told herself, trying to come to terms with the man's blatant disdain.

'He doesn't care.'

'He cares for Henry—otherwise he'd hardly have made the effort to see me in Melbourne.'

It was true. For a busy country doctor to make time in his city visit to try and stir a relative's conscience. . . It spoke of a dedication and caring that were at odds with arrogance.

'Maybe he cares for Henry as much as I care for Paddy.'

Paddy.

At least now she'd see him again—and maybe she'd be able to visit him a couple more times before he died, now that she wasn't going half a world away. Determined to cheer herself a little, Bonnie paid the elderly man a visit.

He was propped up in the ward, his bright eyes jealously devouring other people's visitors. When Bonnie arrived he greeted her with delight.

'Well, would you look at you,' he crowed. 'I'd hardly have recognised you without the white coat. You're a picture, Dr Gaize, and that's the truth.'

Bonnie flushed, her hands self-consciously smoothing the gay print dress she'd put on especially to please him.

'Get on with you,' she laughed. 'You're an old hand at kissing the blarney stone, I reckon.'

Paddy's smile had slipped. He glanced at his bedside clock. 'Shouldn't you be on your way to the airport?' he demanded and his frown deepened as Bonnie told him what had happened.

'So you're missing your holiday because of family obligation and this Dr Halford's standover tactics,' he muttered darkly. 'I hope your uncle appreciates it.'

'If he does I'll hardly know,' Bonnie told him. 'He's a man of few words.' A sudden vision of the silent farmhouse made her catch her breath with dismay.

'So what are you spending your holiday money on?' Paddy demanded and Bonnie looked blank.

'I suppose. . .' She shrugged. She'd been saving for this holiday for so long. She'd scraped to put herself through university and then, two years ago when she'd started working, she'd kept herself on the same harsh regime. She had enough for a truly splendid holiday.

'I suppose I'll put it in my superannuation fund.'

'Superannuation,' Paddy grimaced. 'For heaven's sake, girl. How old are you?'

'Twenty-six.'

'Then get out and do something frivolous,' Paddy ordered. 'So if you get hit by a bus when you're forty you won't lie under the front wheels thinking, I should have spent some of that money! Do you have a car?'

'N. . . No.'

'There you are, then.' He lay back on his pillows and wheezed for a little, his indignation winding him. 'And you're going to the country so you need a car. So go out this morning and buy yourself something really splendid. A Christmas present from you to you, to give yourself some fun despite this Dr Halford and Uncle Henry.' Then he looked at his doctor wistfully. 'And come back and tell me what you bought before you go.'

Something splendid.

Bonnie took herself off to the travel agent, armed with a certificate from a colleague saying she wasn't able to travel because of her uncle's ill health, and cashed in her ticket. Then, clutching a cheque for an almost obscene amount of money, she walked along the High Street.

Something splendid. . .

Bonnie took a deep breath. Paddy's eyes seemed on her and also, inexplicably, those of Webb Halford's.

Webb Halford thought she was a frivolous, uncaring little tramp. Frivolous. . . Bonnie Gaize had never been frivolous in her whole life.

'A Christmas present from you to you,' Paddy had ordered. Bonnie hadn't had a Christmas present for years—not since her aunt stopped wrapping school books and expecting gratitude. And now she was missing the holiday of a lifetime because she couldn't be frivolous.

'So be a little bit silly,' she whispered to herself. 'Just a little——'

A little?

For once in her life, Bonnie Gaize was going to be very, very silly. Dr Bonnie Gaize was going Christmas shopping.

Three hours later, Bonnie approached the bed where Paddy was vainly trying to sleep.

'Want to see my Christmas present to me?' she smiled, touching his arm.

The Irishman jerked into wakefulness. He coughed once, caught his breath and his weary eyes gleamed.

'You haven't. . .' he whispered.

'I have.'

He stared up at her. 'Where is it?'

'In the car park.' She motioned to the wheelchair she was pushing. 'Let's go.'

It took his breath away. Paddy sat in the wheelchair and gazed at the tiny red sports car in awe.

'I've dreamed of owning a car like that,' he whispered, fighting for breath. 'One day—I kept telling myself that one day I'd be rich enough to do it. Only I had to support my mum, and then my brother and his kids needed help. . .' He turned to her then and gripped her hand. 'Good on you, girl.'

Then he glanced back at the ward windows as if expecting Sister to come charging forth and drag him back to his prison. 'You don't suppose. . . You don't reckon you could give me a ride in it, do you?' he asked.

Bonnie smiled. The embryo of an idea which had been floating in her head since Paddy had mentioned a car was fast becoming a full-fledged plan. 'I reckon,' she told him. 'In fact, if you're agreeable, I have a better idea.'

'And. . . And what might that be?'

'I bought this car for one major reason,' Bonnie grinned. 'So I can put you in the passenger seat, strap our luggage on the back and take us both home.'

'Take us both. . .'

'I'm heading for a quiet, quiet Christmas, looking after an uncle I hardly know,' Bonnie told him. 'I thought, if it's OK with you, I might add to the household. How about coming home with me, Paddy Hulbert?'

The Irishman gazed at her blankly, eyes vainly trying to disguise a flare of hope.

'You don't mean it?'

'Why don't I mean it?'

'Because doctors don't take their patients home for Christmas,' Paddy wheezed.

'This one does,' Bonnie told him. She bent to give him a swift hug. 'This one does.'

## CHAPTER TWO

BY RIGHTS, Bonnie should have wept the whole way home. Instead, she drove out of the city in brilliant sunshine, and then turned her nose farmward with a weird sense of anticipation.

It wasn't anything to do with Webb Halford, she told herself as she hummed along to the car radio. It wasn't. . .

Beside her, Paddy sat upright, rigid in expectancy. Bonnie had surrounded him with pillows and his oxygen mask lay beside him in case of need, but there was no way Paddy was letting his illness mar this journey. He knocked back Bonnie's offer of sunburn cream with scorn.

'I'm going to lie in bed for the next couple of days and whinge of sunburn,' he chortled. 'I'm going to feel almost human again.'

Bonnie looked sideways at him and smiled. May this work, she whispered to herself. May this work. . .

Two hours later she pulled into the Kurrara Hospital car park. Kurrara was a small town, and the hospital boasted only two doctors. One of them Bonnie knew from her childhood—old Dr Roberts. Webb Halford was new.

'I hope Dr Roberts is on duty today,' she told Paddy as she brought the little car to a halt.

It wasn't true. For some crazy reason she was hoping with an almost fierce intensity that Webb Halford was here to see her do what he regarded as the right thing.

She gave herself an angry shake. For heaven's sake, Bonnie Gaize. . .

'Shall I take you into Reception while I see my uncle?' she asked Paddy. 'I won't be long. I'll just make arrangements for the ambulance to bring him home tomorrow morning.'

'You're not getting me inside another bloody hospital,' Paddy said darkly. 'Get away with you, girl. I'll sit here and work on my suntan.' He gave a sudden chortle. 'They can't threaten me with skin cancer now, can they?'

Bonnie's uncle was lying flat on his back in a ward by himself. The Christmas decorations seemed incongruous here—the man's loneliness was almost tangible.

'Uncle Henry. . .' Bonnie had meant to walk forward and give him a kiss. Instead, Henry's eyes stopped her in her tracks as he turned to face her. They were almost fearful.

'You. . .' he whispered.

'Yes, it's me.' Bonnie made herself walk forward then and tried to take her uncle's hand. He pulled back as if burned.

'I never thought you'd come.' His voice was a harsh croak.

'No.' She shook her head, making no further move to touch him. 'But Dr Halford says you need me.'

'I don't need you!' He shrank back on his pillows, a big man reduced by pain and despair. 'Dr Halford had no right. . . Bonnie, I'm damned if I'll accept your help.'

'No.' Bonnie nodded. She'd expected nothing less. After the last time she'd been in this man's house—after what had passed between them—well, there was nothing left of a relationship that had been tenuous to begin with. 'I guess you don't want my help.' She took a deep breath. 'But maybe you can help me.'

'Help you. . .?'

'I've a friend in the car,' Bonnie told him. 'A friend who's dying of emphysema. He's an ex-dairy farmer and he's longing to spend his last few weeks on a farm. His last Christmas. So maybe. . . Maybe we can help each other.'

It took longer than she'd hoped and by the time Bonnie finally had her uncle's agreement to her plans she'd left Paddy for too long in the car. She flicked a nervous glance at her watch as she hurried back down the hospital corridor. As she rounded the corner to Reception, Webb Halford stepped out to meet her.

He'd been waiting for her. There was a sheaf of papers on the desk where he had been working, but he'd obviously been warned that Bonnie was in the hospital.

'Well, well,' he said drily as he moved out in front of her. 'The prodigal daughter.'

'You can keep your nasty tongue in your head,' Bonnie retorted, her voice slightly breathless. 'Could you arrange for the ambulance to bring my uncle home in the morning?' He'd have to be transported flat on a stretcher.

'I can do that. Barring emergencies they'll bring him home at about nine.'

'Fine. And now, I'm. . .'

'In a hurry,' he finished for her. 'Ah, yes.'

'I have a friend in the car.'

'Who doesn't like to be kept waiting.' He nodded, staying exactly where he was and effectively blocking her escape route. 'Your friend—he's staying with you?'

The automatic assumption that it was a male friend brought an angry flush to Bonnie's cheeks but she managed to nod.

'Yes.'

'Then I hope he's good at milking cows. The neighbour who's been looking after them rang the hospital this morning to find out what was happening. I said Henry's daughter was coming today and he decided he'd milked for the last time. You and Jacinta don't seem to be flavour of the month around here.'

Bonnie closed her eyes. She'd expected nothing else.

Dairy cows had to be milked twice a day, no matter what catastrophes were happening around them, and in times of trouble the district farmers helped each other.

Not on the Gaizes' farm, though. Aunt Lois had alienated every farmer in the district with her superior air and her poisonous tongue.

Bonnie remembered a farmer coming once to plead for a loan of a tractor because his bull was caught in a bog. Aunt Lois had given the man a lecture on his poor farming techniques and told him he deserved to lose the bull. When Henry protested, Lois had withered him with a look and told him to get on with his milking.

How had Henry taken such treatment all those years? It never made sense to Bonnie, but now, now when Henry himself was in trouble, she wasn't surprised at the neighbour's attitude.

'I'll look after the milking,' she told Webb Halford.

He glanced out the window towards her unsuitable little car—a slash of crimson against the grey of the car-park asphalt. Paddy had his back to the hospital entrance—all they could see was the shock of his still red hair.

'That's what the boyfriend's for, is it?' Webb asked, and Bonnie gritted her teeth. The man was obnoxious.

'That's right,' she muttered. 'Now if you'll excuse me——'

'You realise your uncle can't be left while you milk?' Webb demanded, his hand coming out to restrain her. 'He's totally bedridden, and if he tries to weight bear. . .'

'The bones in his pelvis will shift without setting,' Bonnie said through gritted teeth. 'You don't have to teach me my medicine, Dr Halford. As you said, that's why I brought. . .that's why I brought the boyfriend. Now will you get out of my way?'

The last few words were said with such intensity that he did move. Webb Halford took a step back, looking down at her mounting colour.

'Do you get this angry often, Dr Gaize?' It was asked with detached interest—and once again Bonnie had the impression that she was a rather intriguing form of insect life, to be watched and judged.

'Only when I'm in the company of people I consider arrogant, rude and totally offensive,' she snapped. 'Why you feel you have the right to criticise me——'

'Is it a novel sensation?' he asked, interrupting her. 'To be criticised? You and Jacinta sound as if you had nicely indulged childhoods—and when Henry needs help then one of you refuses absolutely and the other sweeps home reluctantly with sports car and boyfriend in tow——'

'You've said enough,' Bonnie whispered, her colour fading. She dug her fingers so hard into her palms that they hurt. 'You've insulted me in every conceivable way and you haven't one clue what you're talking about, Webb Halford. Tomorrow I'll take my uncle home and I'll do my duty by him; even though I owe him nothing. And then I'll leave again. And I tell you this—I'll leave more than Henry behind when I go. I'll leave you with pleasure. I'm beginning to think that living within thirty miles of an opinionated, bigoted doctor like you will be harder than looking after my uncle. Much harder!'

The short journey out to the farm was done almost in silence. Paddy had looked at Bonnie's face as she emerged from the hospital and wisely held his counsel. He could guess a few things, could Paddy Hulbert, and Bonnie had told him enough on the journey from the city to make his guesses remarkably accurate.

Finally Bonnie stopped at the farm boundary to open the gate.

'I should be doing that,' Paddy said regretfully as she climbed back into the car. He looked around the wide, sweeping paddocks with cows placidly grazing among the trees. 'Eh, Bonnie, it's just as I imagined. . . Just like my place. . .'

'A good place for a man to come home to,' Bonnie smiled and the Irishman nodded.

He fell silent again as Bonnie also gazed across the open paddocks. This, too, had been her home.

Amazingly, it felt good to be here.

Bonnie worked solidly for the rest of the day and by the time she fell into bed that night she was exhausted. She had cleaned the dreary, unloved farmhouse, milked the cows and made Paddy as comfortable as she could. There had been no woman near the farm for two years and it showed.

Paddy was settled into the big room at the back of the house where Jacinta had once slept. It held two beds, and Bonnie made them both up.

'It's going to be a hospital ward,' she told Paddy, setting up the intercom she had brought from Melbourne. 'While I milk, you and my uncle will look after each other. I can hear what's going on and you'll be able to yell if there's any reason for me to come in a hurry.'

It was the best she could do. By rights Paddy should be in a hospital ward with constant supervision, but as Bonnie had struggled in the dairy with her endless stream of cows, intercom rigged up above her head, she had known what Paddy preferred. The French windows in his room looked right out over the farm.

'He'll even get to smell cow dung,' she thought wearily as she climbed, exhausted, into her narrow childhood bed.

'So maybe it'll be OK.' Bonnie put her face into the pillow with a sigh. Seven hours of sleep and then the cows would need milking again.

'Some holiday.'

Her eyes shut tight on the thought.

By the time the milk tanker had left the yard at nine the next morning, Bonnie had been up for almost four hours. She'd milked seventy-three cows, sluiced down the dairy, prepared breakfast—though she still couldn't get Paddy to eat—and subjected him to a bed bath.

'So we'll have you smelling of roses to meet my uncle Henry,' she teased him as she adjusted his bedclothes, then looked up and out the window at the sound of an approaching vehicle. The ambulance was right on time.

She walked out to meet it, conscious suddenly of her grubby jeans and T-shirt. She hardly looked an antiseptic nurse to be greeting her patient; but then an antiseptic hospital atmosphere was hardly what either Paddy or Henry wanted.

Though who knew what Henry really wanted? He had stopped saying what he wanted a score of years before.

The ambulance drew to a halt under the gums. An officer jumped from the driver's seat and opened the rear doors wide. Webb Halford stepped from the interior and looked around him.

If anything the man looked more at home in this farm environment than he had in the hospital. In a short-sleeved, open-necked shirt and casual trousers, with his face tanned and his eyes narrowed against the harsh summer sun, he looked more of a farmer than a doctor. Bonnie had to blink to make herself accept that this man was a colleague.

A doctor. No more and no less. The air of authority around him was false. He had no more authority here than she did—in fact a lot less!

She pushed her shoulders back in an automatic gesture of defiance and walked over to the ambulance.

'You're on time.' It was a matter of finding something to say—anything.

'I try to be reliable.' Once again there was that distinct slur to his words—an edge that made the comment cutting.

Bonnie bit her lip. This man had judged her and found her wanting.

'The boyfriend finished milking yet?' he asked and it was as much as Bonnie could do not to walk over and slap his arrogant face.

'Hours ago. Could you please help take my uncle inside and then leave as fast as possible?'

'You don't relish intrusion on your privacy?'

'No, I don't.'

'You realise I intend dropping in periodically to check on my patient?'

'There's no need,' Bonnie hissed. 'We don't need you.'

'I'm your uncle's doctor and he wishes me to visit. Are you saying you don't permit it?'

Bonnie counted to a silent ten. When she finished she had herself under control, but by the sardonic grin on Webb Halford's face he knew just how tenuous her grip on her temper was. It was as if the man was baiting her—and enjoying it.

'I have no control over the visitors my uncle sees on his own farm,' she said, through gritted teeth. 'Are you planning on leaving him in the ambulance all day or will you bring him through?'

To her annoyance Webb Halford had ignored her. He and the ambulance officer had already climbed into the van, and now emerged, carefully manoeuvring Uncle Henry out into the open.

'Hi, Uncle Henry,' Bonnie told the man on the stretcher, swallowing her anger. 'Welcome. . . welcome home.'

The injured man gazed at her blankly and then turned away. Bonnie stared. She wasn't imagining it. There were tears in her uncle's eyes.

'Bring him through here,' she said in a voice that wasn't quite steady. She led the way through the kitchen garden and into the house.

When they reached the passage on the other side of the kitchen, Webb automatically started turning left.

'Not that way,' Bonnie said quickly. 'Uncle, I hope you don't mind but I've set up the back bedroom for you. It'll be easier for us all if you're in there.'

'Leaving Henry's bedroom and double bed for you and the boyfriend,' Webb said drily. 'I suppose I should have thought of that.'

Bonnie flushed bright crimson. Once again her fingers clenched into her palms. The thought of sleeping in Aunt Lois' bed made her feel ill. She never would. . .

'The big bed is low and spongy,' she said tartly. 'I've put slats on the higher single bed in the back bedroom.'

'How very professional.'

Bonnie ignored him. She walked forward and swung the back bedroom door wide. Webb Halford bore his end of the stretcher through and then stopped in shock. Paddy was sitting propped up with pillows, expectantly waiting.

Anything new in Paddy's world was an event to be

savoured, and this was interesting. He'd been in the same hospital ward for two months. Now he had a new place, a new doctor, a new ward mate and an ambulance officer to check out. The journey yesterday had exhausted him more than he cared to admit, but he was missing nothing for all of it.

'Top of the morning to ye,' he said in broad Irish and then collapsed into a fit of coughing. Concerned, Bonnie walked forward and fitted the oxygen mask.

'Just relax and go with it, Paddy,' she told him gently. 'Don't let it scare you. Slow, deep breaths.'

There was absolute silence in the room while Paddy slowly recovered. Webb looked like a man struck by lightning.

'Are you going to put me down?' It was finally Henry who broke the silence, and Webb looked down at the man he was carrying.

'Do you know who this is, Henry?'

'Yeah.' Like Paddy, Henry was at the edge of exhaustion and it showed. 'He's a friend of Bonnie's.' He turned his head to look at the suffering Irishman. 'And he's a welcome guest.'

There was no mistaking the defiance of that tone. It was as if Henry was standing up to the two-year-dead Lois. At last. . .

'A friend of Bonnie's. . .' Webb's penetrating eyes took in the Irishman, the oxygen mask and cylinder, the gauntness of the man's face and shallowness of his breathing, and the colour of his hair. 'This—this was the man I saw yesterday. The man in your car. . .'

'Yes.' Bonnie held the mask for a further moment, and then Paddy took it himself, motioning to her that the worst was over. 'Could you put Henry on the bed, please? He's not too comfortable there.'

For a supremely satisfactory moment the arrogant Webb Halford was discomposed. He stared from

Paddy to Bonnie and back again.

'Put him on the bed, please,' Bonnie said gently and it was the ambulance officer who grinned and moved first to do her bidding.

'What the hell do you think you're playing at?' Webb demanded. Webb Halford was way off-balance and it showed.

He was still moving automatically with the ambulance officer, skilfully laying Henry on the bed and manoeuvring the stretcher from beneath him. Bonnie was ready with the covers, pulling them up to cover her uncle. She didn't answer until she had Henry tucked in, as comfortable as she could make him.

'I don't think I understand the question,' she said at last. She straightened and met Webb's gaze squarely.

'You brought this man——'

'This man——' Bonnie turned to Paddy and smiled down at him '—this is Paddy Hulbert—my friend. He's ill and my uncle's agreed to have him here while they both convalesce.'

Webb's eyes took in the oxygen cylinder and mask, and Paddy's gaunt, emaciated face.

'What's wrong with you?' he asked bluntly. Paddy was in his late sixties—too young to look like this through age.

Paddy laid down the mask and grinned across at Bonnie. He sensed undercurrents here, and he was a man to relish a few undercurrents.

'Emphysema,' he whispered huskily. 'And a gammy leg. I'm not long for this world, I reckon, but Doc Gaize—Bonnie here—reckoned I might be more at peace with my Maker among a bit of cow dung.' He smiled across at Henry. 'You're lucky to have a kid like this for a niece, I reckon.'

Henry said nothing. His tired eyes crossed to Bonnie and then away, looking anywhere but at her.

'If that's all, Dr Halford,' Bonnie said pointedly, 'I expect you've work to do.' It was a clear dismissal and meant as such.

'I'll talk to you first,' Webb said through gritted teeth.

'Sure,' Bonnie said pleasantly. 'Fire away.'

'Outside.' It was an order. 'Alone!'

'Sounds just like a lover's spat to me,' Paddy told the silent Henry. 'What do you reckon?'

It was all Bonnie could do not to choke on laughter at his words. Then she looked up into Webb's grim face and the laughter died.

'Sure,' she said softly. 'Paddy, behave yourself while I'm gone.'

'Would I be doing anything else?' the Irishman demanded. He shrugged his shoulders and coughed again. 'I had thought of indulging in an orgy or two for a couple of minutes but if you say not then——' he picked up his mask again '—I guess I'll just have to practise my breathing instead.'

Bonnie and Webb walked silently back out through the house. After one look at Dr Halford's face, the ambulance officer had wisely gone ahead. By the time they emerged from the back door, the officer was already in his vehicle, his radio's music sounding vaguely discordant against the peace of the farm. Above their heads, the magpies in the surrounding eucalypts warbled hard in protest.

Bonnie hardly heard. She was conscious only of Webb.

'Now, would you tell me what the hell is going on?' Webb demanded as the screen door swung closed behind them.

'Why should I?' It was a petty response, but then Bonnie was feeling distinctly petty. This man made her feel cheap and contemptible.

'Is this another relation?'

'You mean, am I killing two birds with the one stone?' Bonnie gave a mirthless laugh. 'Having been hounded to do my duty by one relation, you think I might shove in another for good measure. Next you'll be accusing me of knocking them off with cyanide for some imagined inheritance.'

Silence. It went on and on. Bonnie gazed around her at the sun-scorched paddocks. She wasn't going to help him out of this in a million years.

Finally Webb spoke, and when he did his voice sounded tired—as though he no longer understood and he no longer cared. 'Is he dying?' His thoughts were obviously still on Paddy.

'I don't know.'

'He has emphysema?'

'Yes.' Bonnie shrugged. 'But it wasn't life-threatening until he broke his leg. Since then—well, after two months of traction and with nothing to look forward to, Paddy's decided he wants to die.'

'Do you want him to?'

It was a bland, hard question and it book Bonnie's breath away. She wheeled to face him.

'What sort of a question is that, Webb Halford?' she whispered. 'Paddy Hulbert is my friend, and my patient.'

'But he has nothing to look forward to.'

'No.' Bonnie bit her lip. 'Unless. . .'

'Unless what?'

Bonnie shrugged. 'Unless I can pull off a miracle.' She took a deep breath. 'A Christmas miracle. That's what I'm aiming for, Dr Halford. Crazy, you might say, but I'd rather be categorised as crazy than as a self-centred, uncaring little tart, which you seem to think me. Now, if you'll excuse me. . .'

'How do you think you'll look after them?'

Bonnie tilted her small chin. 'That's my business, Dr Halford.'

'Your uncle's my patient.'

'He's home now. Do you suppose he'll agree to go back into hospital if you say so?'

'He might,' Webb said heavily. 'He was reluctant to come home this morning.'

Bonnie bit her lip. Of course. She hadn't worked her miracle yet.

'I'll manage.'

'How?'

He turned to stare down at her—this stained and grubby waif of a doctor who seemed like no doctor he had ever met. There were things going on here he didn't understand, but Webb Halford's face said that at least he was suspending judgement for a while. He wanted to know.

'It's not perfect,' Bonnie told him reluctantly. 'I know it's not. I have to milk and there'll be times when I have to leave them. But I've put the intercom and the telephone between them, and I take the other end of the intercom with me. Paddy's able to stand for a little—only briefly but I hope that'll improve if I can persuade him to eat. So——'

'They should have full-time nursing care.'

'I know. They both should be in hospital. But in hospital they'll both die. So. . . So this is the best I can do.'

'And you always do the best you can do?' It was a wry question, but not quite as insulting as it might have been. The doubt in Webb Halford's eyes said that he was starting to reassess. She just might. . .

'Always,' Bonnie said, her voice falling away so that Webb was struggling to hear. 'That is, when I'm permitted. And you're preventing me now, Dr Halford.

I think. . .I think it's time for you to leave.'

'To let you get on with creating your miracles?'

'I hope so,' Bonnie whispered. 'I certainly hope so.'

# CHAPTER THREE

THE rest of the day passed in a whirl of activity. Every time Bonnie took a breath there were things waiting to be done.

It was Saturday. Today Bonnie should be landing at Heathrow. Instead she was hanging out lines and lines of dripping laundry. Apart from the few things Henry used, the linen in this place hadn't been aired since her aunt's death, and Bonnie was darned if she was putting musty sheets on her patients' beds.

Afterwards Bonnie grilled sausages for lunch, then took back Paddy's untouched plate and washed it in grim silence. At least Henry was eating, even if he wasn't talking to her. She returned to their temporary ward to give both patients a massage, and before she knew it, it was time for milking again.

Seventy-two cows. . .

Hadn't there been seventy-three this morning?

Three hours later Bonnie milked her last cow and then stood at the dairy door, staring down the valley into the gathering night. The cows came up of their own accord. Somewhere below was the missing cow, but Bonnie couldn't go searching now. She had dinner to prepare and her patients to settle.

Why hadn't the cow come up? Bonnie knew what dairy cattle were worth and Henry could ill afford to lose one. Worried, she sluiced down the dairy, then detoured via the hen house before returning to the house.

It was hardly a gourmet meal, Bonnie thought half

an hour later, grimacing as Paddy pushed away his untouched plate.

'You don't like my omelette?'

Paddy shook his head. 'I'm just not hungry, girl.'

'Well, you bloody well ought to be.' It was Henry from the other bed and the sound of his voice made them both jump. He'd hardly spoken since he arrived. Now he was watching Bonnie's worried face, but as she turned to him he turned away and stared straight at Paddy. 'If I'm not mistaken,' he told Paddy, 'this omelette's made from our own chook eggs produced right here on the farm. Isn't that right, lass?'

Bonnie flushed. Lass. . . How long since Henry had called her that? Still he wasn't looking at her.

'I collected them on the way from the dairy,' Bonnie managed to smile. 'Six brown eggs, straight from the girls.'

'My chooks are mostly Rhode Island Reds,' Henry declared. 'There's one though. . .' He paused as though his voice wasn't quite used to working. 'There's one Wyandotte. Frankie, I call her, because when I first got her Johnnie, our rooster, didn't have eyes for any other chook but her. I can't say I blamed him. She's a little beauty—a lovely black and white pedigree. I took her for a debt and if ever I want a special treat I give myself her eggs.' He smiled shyly up at Bonnie. 'You'll pick her. She stands out from the bunch with her colour and smaller size, and her eggs are lighter and creamier.'

A black and white hen. . . Bonnie's heart sank. She'd just locked up the hens and she hadn't seen a black and white bird among the sea of brown poultry. So as well as missing a cow she was now down one chook.

'I guess the neighbour must have been collecting the eggs.' Bonnie hedged for time. 'I think you'll have to make do with Rhode Island eggs tonight.'

'Well, they're pretty good.' Her uncle motioned to Paddy. 'Don't you tell me you're not hungry when you haven't even tasted my girls' eggs. Get yourself around a bit of omelette and then tell me you don't want it.'

Paddy looked from Henry to Bonnie and back again. They were both staring straight at him—daring him to eat. Reluctantly he pulled the plate back.

'Well, I'll have a taste,' he agreed. He cut off a corner and nibbled.

'For Pete's sake, man, you don't eat it like it's caviar,' Henry exploded. 'Get it down you.'

Bonnie held her breath. She had tried so hard to persuade Paddy to eat. Could Henry succeed where everyone else had failed?

To her astonishment Paddy was slicing himself a bigger bite. Henry's eyes watched him, hawklike, as the omelette slowly went down. Slowly. . . Slowly. . .

And finally the plate was clean.

'There,' Henry said in satisfaction. 'Didn't I tell you it was the best?'

'It was OK,' Paddy said dubiously, wiping his mouth. Then he looked up at Bonnie and grinned. 'Well, it was more than OK, really.'

'It didn't smell like antiseptic either,' Bonnie smiled. She looked ruefully down at her stained jeans. 'I've not a trace of antiseptic in sight, more's the pity.' She picked up Paddy's plate, trying to suppress a grin of sheer relief. 'OK, you two. Thirty minutes to read or chat and then lights out.'

'You'd think you'd come to boarding school instead of coming home,' Paddy groaned to Henry but Henry had said all he intended. Paddy shrugged and turned on the radio.

'I'll be back in a moment.' Bonnie hesitated, her hands full of dishes. 'Uncle, we're milking seventy-three cows at the moment, aren't we?'

She had Henry's attention at once.

'Yes,' he said brusquely. 'Why? Are any missing?'

'I haven't been counting,' Bonnie lied. 'But I thought it was about time I did.'

The telephone rang as she left the bedroom. Bonnie picked it up and flinched at the sound of Webb Halford's voice. Why did the man unsettle her so?

'I'm just ringing to check things are OK,' he told her. 'Do you need anything? Are you alright for medications? I'm coming out first thing tomorrow and I can bring anything you need.'

'I'm fine,' Bonnie told him, trying hard to keep her voice even. 'There's no need to come. I'm coping just fine and we don't need you.'

'I'm coming whether you need me or not, Dr Gaize,' Webb told her firmly. 'I'll see you in the morning.'

Darn Webb Halford. She'd almost calmed down again—and now. . . Her hand was trembling as she replaced the receiver and for the life of her Bonnie couldn't figure out why. It was a curt, official telephone call. Not a call to make her feel flustered and. . .

And what?

And vulnerable. That was how Webb Halford made her feel. Young, vulnerable and scared.

She was being silly. There were more important things to be thinking about than Webb Halford.

Like one missing cow.

So where was the dratted creature?

Bonnie walked to the back door and stood looking out over the darkened valley. She could hardly leave her two patients and search now. In the dark it could take her hours.

'Let's hope she appears in the morning,' she whispered. 'Please. . . And while you're at it, could you send a chook home, too?'

Of course neither arrived. Bonnie counted her cows with even more care during the next morning's milking but as the last cow moved into the bails she sighed. Seventy-two.

OK. It was daylight and she'd worked out a near-foolproof alarm system.

The two farm dogs, Bindy and Dougal, had hardly left Bonnie's side since she arrived. They were placid collies and she'd only seen them upset once—when she and Paddy had been testing the intercom.

'Bonnie,' Paddy had yelled into the machine. The sound had reverberated through the dairy and both dogs almost went wild trying to reach the intercom above their heads. Their barking could be heard from one end of the farm to the other.

Bonnie cleaned down the dairy, tied both dogs immediately under the intercom and hauled out the farm's three-wheel bike-cum-tractor. She could be down in the bottom paddock in minutes, and up again if the barking started.

Three-quarters of the way down the track Bonnie found what she was looking for, and the find gave her no joy at all.

The cow had slipped on a steep incline as she took a short cut from paddock to path. She lay on her side, her huge brown eyes rolling pitifully, and it took Bonnie only seconds to realise what the problem was.

Her leg lay at an impossible angle. Obviously, every time she stood the leg gave under her again. The cow tried to rise as Bonnie approached, managed to drag herself a few feet and then sank again with a bovine moan.

'Easy, girl. . .'

Abandoning the bike, Bonnie started forward. The last thing she wanted was to make the injured animal haul herself away. 'Easy. . .'

It took patience. Henry was the only human these cows knew and the pain-racked cow was now frightened as well. She kept trying to heave herself up as Bonnie inched forward. Finally the cow abandoned the attempt. Clearly, whatever Bonnie intended couldn't be worse than the pain in the cow's leg.

Slowly Bonnie bent, her hands running over the injured animal. For the leg to be at such an impossible angle then it must be broken—and there wasn't much future for a cow with a broken leg. She felt again, frowning in frustration at her lack of knowledge of cow anatomy. If this was a human then she'd say the leg was dislocated.

Finally, Bonnie squatted back on her heels, considering her options. She had a cow with a dislocated back leg, and this cow was one of Henry's best young animals. It didn't need skill to see that.

So?

So she needed a vet, and fast. This wasn't a disaster; with skill, dislocated legs could be corrected. She'd have to tell Henry and find out who he used.

Bonnie made her way swiftly on foot up to the house to find her patients deep in altercation. Despite her haste, Bonnie hesitated, melting back out of sight of the door.

'It's no use your telling me you're not Mick,' Henry was informing the man in the other bed. 'With carrot hair and a name like Paddy you can hardly be anything else. And it's your radio. So we'll turn on your priests or whatever and let 'em do their worst. If they succeed in converting me, well, good luck to 'em.'

'But you're Presbyterian, mate,' Paddy protested. 'And it's your house. So we'll listen to a few ministers and elders from yon kirk. It won't kill me for once—I might even learn something.'

'But it's your radio. . .' Henry was becoming heated.

'Alright. . .' Clearly the argument had been going on for some time and Paddy had had enough. The Irishman fiddled with the dials of his radio. 'Tell you what. We'll sit on the fence. Here's a solemn sounding service from the Greek Orthodox lot. Maybe they'll convert the pair of us.'

Despite her distress, Bonnie choked on laughter. She walked in and smiled down at her two patients.

'OK, you heathens,' she started, 'I need help.'

'Heathens. . .' They both glared and Bonnie grinned as she walked over to Henry's bed.

'Henry, I need to know who your vet is,' she told him and watched the lightness fade from his face.

'I don't have one.'

Bonnie frowned. 'But. . .but all farmers have a vet they can call on. It used to be old Doc Davis. Is he still around?'

'He had a heart attack three months ago,' Henry said grimly, all trace of laughter gone. 'Nearest vet is forty miles away and he won't do calls. What's the problem?'

Bonnie sighed and dug her hands into her jeans. There was no easy way out of this.

'One of your young cows has dislocated her leg,' she told him and her uncle's face set.

'Which one?'

'A little Jersey with a white face and one white ear.'

He groaned. 'It'd have to be her. She's a little beauty.'

'So—who do I call?'

'You don't.' Henry's voice was clipped and hard. 'There's a gun on top of my bedroom wardrobe and there are cartridges in the bedside table. You'll have to shoot her.'

'Shoot her. . .' Bonnie stared blankly at her uncle. 'But. . . But I can't. . .'

'Then you'll have to watch her die slowly,' the elderly farmer whispered. His eyes met Bonnie's, bleak and cold. 'I should have taught you to shoot when you were a kid.'

'There's. . . There's no choice?'

'You'll never get the vet here. Not one hope in heck. It's even Sunday, to boot. You'll be lucky if you can get them to answer the phone.'

'But. . . But that means I have to take her to the vet. . . Doesn't it?'

'No. She'd be dead of pain and shock long before you got there—even supposing you could winch her onto the trailer by yourself, which you couldn't. No.' He turned his face away. 'Go and get the gun and I'll show you what you have to do.'

It was a lesson Bonnie had never wanted. Ten minutes later she emerged from the house feeling sick to the stomach.

'And somehow you're going to have to bury her, girl,' Henry had added. 'You can't leave a dead cow on the track. . .' His voice shook with weariness and distress. 'You shouldn't be here. I knew you shouldn't be here. . .'

There was no way either of her two patients could help. It was bad enough that they had to know what she was doing. Bonnie gripped her gun as if it was threatening to explode at any moment and started walking across the yard to the track. She was so intent on her grim task that she hardly noticed a big grey car pull into the yard and stop.

'Where on earth do you think you're going with that?'

Webb Halford. She'd know that voice anywhere. She had almost forgotten that he was coming.

Bonnie stopped dead but didn't turn. She couldn't. This was the hardest task she had ever been asked to perform. Ever.

'Are you going to answer me?' He strode across the yard to where she stood, his attention focused solely on the gun.

'I've just shot my two patients and now I'm off to find a few neighbours,' Bonnie managed, responding to the accusing tone. Her quiet response was strung tight. Webb Halford would have to be a fool not to hear the pressure behind the words.

She didn't turn to look at him. Bonnie stayed where she was, eyes staring sightlessly down the valley as she tried to block out what was ahead. She didn't move as Webb reached her and firmly took the gun from her hand.

'I have to. . .' she whispered.

'Shoot a few neighbours?' There was both concern and mystification in Webb's voice. 'Let's see—there's Mr and Mrs Travis. They have seven horrible children. You could shoot a few, end up in jail yourself and the Travises wouldn't notice the difference. They'd just have a few more to fill the empty beds.' He broke the gun open and removed the cartridge. 'Not worth the effort, I'd say. Leave the Travises to deal with their own ghastly children.'

'Please. . .' Bonnie's voice broke. 'Please put the cartridge back in. I don't know how. . .'

'Not until you tell me what you intend doing with it.'

'I have to shoot a cow.'

'Oh.' Webb's eyes softened to understanding. He didn't load the gun again, but slipped the cartridge in his pocket and turned Bonnie round to face him. His firm hands on her shoulders brooked no opposition. 'Why?'

The sudden softening of his voice undermined

Bonnie's strength. Not that she had much anyway, but she had enough to do what she must. Now. . . Now it was as much as she could do to fight back tears. Webb Halford stood, looking down at her, and she felt like sinking onto his chest and weeping.

For heaven sake! This man thought her little more than he thought of a maw worm—and a rather repulsive maw worm at that. She made herself look up at him. In his weekend gear—checked, open-necked shirt and jeans—he was impossibly handsome. The sort of man Jacinta would die for. Not the sort of man to give comfort to Bonnie.

'A cow. . .' She gulped, striving for words. 'She's dislocated her leg. I can't get it back in and my uncle says there's no vet.' She looked up at him, half-hopeful that he'd shake his head and say her uncle was wrong. Instead he nodded grimly.

'Your uncle's right. There's been no vet in the valley for three months and the farmers are at their wits' end. The current vet refuses to sell his surgery as he thinks he'll come back eventually. No other vet will set up because if Davis comes back there'll be no work. So we're at an impasse.'

'I see.' Bonnie pulled away from his hold and, reluctantly it seemed, Webb let her go. 'So I really do have to shoot her?'

'No.' Webb shook his head and his eyes softened. Bonnie's fear of what she had to do was almost palpable. 'If it's necessary, then I'll shoot her,' he told her.

Bonnie took a deep breath. This man was her enemy. He'd insulted her in every conceivable way. She shouldn't accept his help.

She shouldn't. . .'

'Please,' she whispered at last. 'I don't think. . .' She shook her head. 'I'm so scared that I'll falter. Make her suffer even more. . .'

'I won't miss,' Webb promised, his eyes still holding their strange softness. He held out his hand and took Bonnie's in his, tightening his hold when Bonnie pulled back in shock. 'Take me to her, Bonnie.'

'Not Bonnie. Dr. . . Dr Gaize,' Bonnie whispered helplessly and Webb laughed, a strong, rich laugh which enveloped both of them.

'When you're acting like a Dr Gaize then I'll call you Dr Gaize,' he promised. 'With your freckles and your big scared eyes you look like no doctor I've ever met. So—when you're acting like a Bonnie, then I'll call you just that.'

The cow was still lying where Bonnie had left her. This time as Bonnie and Webb approached she didn't stir. The pain was starting to overwhelm her.

'How long has she been like this?' Webb bent over her with a frown.

'I'm not sure. At least. . .at least since last night. She didn't come for milking and I found her this morning.'

'You didn't look last night?'

Bonnie flushed. 'I couldn't.'

'Of course. The conscientious Dr Gaize had patients to look after.' It was a wry, almost insulting remark, but Webb's heart wasn't in insulting Bonnie. His mind was very firmly on the job in hand. Strong hands were running skilfully over the cow's leg, and he spoke softly to the animal as his fingers probed.

'OK,' he said at last. 'It's dislocated alright. I can't feel any breaks.'

'It might just as well be broken,' Bonnie said bleakly. 'For all we can do about it.'

'Don't be too sure.'

'What. . .what do you mean?'

'I mean I've been acting vet for this valley for the last three months.'

'You mean. . .' Bonnie stared at him. 'You mean you know how to deal with this?'

'I know the theory,' Webb grimaced. He glanced up at Bonnie's shocked face and shrugged. 'Oh, I'm no vet. But there have been a few occasions when I've been the only one capable of doing a fast Caesarian or setting a dog's hind leg. So—I've made a few urgent phone calls, read a few texts and learned a bit of basic veterinarian medicine.' He moved to the cow's head and touched the animal gently between the rolling eyes. 'Like what to give you to put you under,' he told the cow.

'You can anaesthetise her?'

'I can hardly try to put that leg in without knocking her out. She'd die of shock if I did.' Webb stood and crossed to the farm bike. 'Stay with her and I'll get what I need.'

He was back in moments, the farm bike laden with heavy ropes and a huge black bag.

'My medical bag,' Webb told Bonnie with wry humour. 'I remember city practice where I carried a bag a size of a briefcase. Now I carry a bag so big I almost need a wheelbarrow to shift it—and my luggage compartment's full of stuff ranging from oxygen cylinders to calving overalls.'

'A jack of all trades,' Bonnie said in amazement, watching him flick open his bag and search for a syringe. The needle he produced made her gasp.

'The vet from Framlirra lent me this,' Webb told her. 'He was sick of being hauled over here in the middle of the night, and finally refused to come. The farmers persuaded me to try and make the man change his mind—and all I got was the offer of equipment. So——' he shrugged his shoulders '—so it's better than nothing.'

'For the farmers maybe,' Bonnie said dubiously.

'But——' She stared at him. Bonnie knew the other doctor in the town—Webb's partner. Old Dr Roberts had never put himself out, even in his younger days. 'You'll be run off your feet,' she whispered. 'How can you be both vet and doctor?'

'I am a bit busy,' Webb admitted, measuring anaesthetic into the syringe. He glanced up at Bonnie's shocked face. 'But it keeps me off the streets. And I charge like a wounded bull. Especially farmers who drive brand new sports cars. Now, let's get on with this, shall we, Dr Gaize?'

The cow was asleep in seconds. As she sank into unconsciousness, Webb moved into position. He pushed his hands round the dislocated joint, feeling where he wanted it to go. 'OK, Dr Gaize,' he told her. 'I want you to pull.'

He showed her how, explaining briefly what they were trying to do and how the leg had to be extended if it were to slip into position. Then Webb sat down in the mud and placed both hands on the cow's dislocated joint. As Bonnie pulled it was up to him to guide the limb safely in position. If she could pull hard enough. . .

She couldn't.

Webb attached ropes to the hock to give extra grip but there was no way Bonnie had the strength needed to shift the limb. The leg stayed exactly where it was.

'If you showed me how to manoeuvre the limb then you could pull,' Bonnie said doubtfully and Webb shook his head.

'Not possible, unless we spend an hour showing you diagrams—and even then I don't think you're strong enough. And shock's taking its toll already. No.' He stared across at the farm bike. 'We get ourselves some horsepower.'

'Horsepower. . .' Bonnie stared at the small tractor.

'You're kidding,' she whispered. 'We'd just pull her along the ground.'

'Not if we anchored her.' Webb looked around him, his eyes lighting on a nearby gum tree. 'That's what I brought the extra rope for. Let's go.'

'You mean. . . You mean you tie her to the tree, and then pull with the tractor?'

'Nearly right,' Webb told her, intent on his task. 'Only it's you who pulls with the tractor. I'll have to stand right here and manoeuvre the limb back when you pull it free from its present position.'

'But what if I pull too hard?'

'Then we break her leg and we'll have to shoot her,' Webb said flatly. 'So I want you to pull slowly—more carefully than you've ever driven a vehicle in your life. Any attempts to drive like a racing driver can be put out of your head now. For once—for once you're going to have to restrain yourself.'

Bonnie bit her lip. She looked up at Webb's face, intent on attaching his ropes.

'This is the only way?'

'This is the only way.'

Bonnie climbed onto the tractor-bike with a sinking heart. No medical training had ever prepared her for this—to pull a leg into position with a tractor. She shifted the machine into gear and then inched forward, her hand unsteady on the unfamiliar controls. Slowly, slowly, the slack on the rope was taken up.

It was so much harder than it sounded—to edge a machine forward a fraction of an inch at a time. One jolt and the leg could snap. Bonnie concentrated fiercely on what she was doing, her eyes half on the rope and half on the controls. The rope had to stay tight. . .tighter. . .

Behind her the cow shifted and Webb yelled. The ropes were anchoring her to the gum tree but Webb was hauling her into the position he wanted, his hands on the leg, pulling it forward and down. He was making sure Bonnie's efforts were directed to hauling the leg back into position and not into an even worse dislocation.

Slowly. . .slowly. . . Bonnie was almost screaming with anxiety and impatience. She held the machine back with exaggerated care, her lips forming a soundless prayer. Please. . . Please. . .

Then a slight slackening of the rope. . .a shout from Webb to back off. Bonnie reversed, taking tension from the rope, and looked back, not daring to hope. Webb's hands were moving frantically and while Bonnie watched, the leg shifted forward, down and slid home.

Dear heaven. . .

Bonnie cut the motor and walked back with legs that would hardly hold her. The cow, still heavily unconscious, lay as if there was nothing wrong with her. Webb flashed a grin up at the girl above him.

'I reckon we've won,' he whispered. He'd used sheer strength to manoeuvre the leg and his voice was laced with exhaustion.

Bonnie slumped down in the mud beside him. It had rained a little the night before and the dust had turned to slush where the cows had plodded up the track. The mud stuck like glue but Bonnie couldn't care less. She looked down at the little cow and her eyes shone. She couldn't have been more pleased than if she'd just saved the life of a human patient.

'Oh, thank you. . .' she whispered. She leaned forward and touched the cow's leg as if she were dreaming. 'Thank you.'

'She'll still need care.'

Webb was looking at the woman beside him strangely. There was a streak of mud down her cheek,

Bonnie knew. She could feel it caking dry. She swiped at it with the back of her hand, realising as she did that she was just spreading it further.

'It'll be best if we could get her up to the house paddock before she wakes,' Webb continued finally. 'I'd rather she was on level ground.'

Bonnie nodded. 'If. . .if you're still willing to help. . .'

'I'm still willing to help,' he told her, and Bonnie flushed at the gentleness of his tone.

Fifteen minutes later the thing was done. Bonnie took the little tractor up to the shed and attached the low trailer. She'd seen her uncle do this time and time again. A rubber mat, thick enough to act as a ramp, rolled from the back. Between them, Bonnie and Webb hauled the mat underneath the unconscious cow, roped her on and then winched her up onto the trailer. They let her down in the lush home paddock behind the house. Here she could wake and move around without being jostled by the other cows.

Webb stood and watched as Bonnie milked dry the little cow's udder. The udder was swollen with milk and if she wasn't drained then she could have milk fever to contend with as well as a sore leg.

Finally Bonnie rose, and as she did the cow's eyes flickered open, rolling in sudden alarm.

'Leave her.' Webb pulled Bonnie back. 'She needs to lie there until she's ready to get up—not get up because she's frightened.' He took Bonnie's hand and drew her fast back out the gate. The tractor was left where it stood. It could be retrieved later.

The feel of Webb's hand was doing strange things to Bonnie. She let her hand lie in his as he opened the gate and ushered her through, anxious not to appear ungracious by pulling it away. . .

Anxious not to pull away. . .

It was a strange sensation. It was a feeling of being cared for—a feeling as novel as it was extraordinary. The warmth from his hand crept through her entire body and she ventured a look up at him. To her confusion he was looking down at her, his eyes filled with the laughter she'd always suspected they could contain.

'Do you know you have mud on your nose, Dr Gaize?' he asked with mock severity and Bonnie smiled shyly at him.

'I guess I have mud everywhere. If Theatre Sister could see me now. . .'

'Country practice isn't like city medicine,' Webb agreed. 'Now, I came to see your human patients. Shouldn't we check them after so long?'

To her surprise there was no censure in his tone—no hint that she'd been negligent in leaving them. Despite that, Bonnie hastily told him her set-up with her intercom dog alarm and Webb's laughter deepened.

'A resourceful lady, if ever I met one.' His eyes on hers were warm with admiration and Bonnie felt herself flush all over. She was starting to feel herself drift into something she'd never experienced before.

And didn't want to. She gave herself an angry mental shake. There was no joy down the road her errant heart was leading her. Don't forget who you are, Bonnie Gaize, she told herself crossly. You're not Jacinta.

'I'll go in and see them now,' Webb was saying, ignorant of the feelings his smile was causing. 'Have you any problems?'

'Not if you can find me a chook,' Bonnie managed and saw Webb's smile slip.

'I beg your pardon?'

'My uncle's favourite hen has taken herself off,' Bonnie explained. 'And I don't know how to tell him.'

'You've looked?' Thankfully Webb didn't belittle her concern. He knew as well as Bonnie that to bed-bound patients small tragedies assumed gigantic proportions. At least they could report the recovery of a cow.

'If she was here she'd be in the poultry run. The only thing is. . .'

'Yes?'

'The neighbour didn't lock them up at night,' Bonnie said slowly. 'They wandered in and out at will. Most of the chooks are bigger than the missing one. She'd have been easy prey for a fox.'

'I see.' Webb frowned. 'And you don't want to tell your uncle?'

'No, I don't.' Bonnie bit her lip. 'He's. . .he's depressed enough already. He'll know she's gone as he's already looking for her eggs. If I could just get him on his feet first before I tell him she's been taken—so he thinks things are going to get better. . .'

'I see what you mean.' Once again Webb was looking at her with that strange expression, as though he was reassessing and was stunned at what he saw. 'Why don't you tell him she's gone broody?'

'Broody. . .'

'If a hen's broody then she's off the lay,' Webb explained. 'It can last about six weeks—so he won't expect any eggs from her. Then, maybe the day before he's ready to walk out to the yard she can quietly depart this mortal coil after a quick dose of something like chook flu.' He grinned. 'I'll substantiate the diagnosis myself, if you like. We'll work like navvies to save her life—every marvel of modern medicine—but——' he spread his hands in a gesture of fatality '—sometimes even we doctors have to learn we're not invincible. Poor chook. . .!'

Bonnie choked on a laugh. 'You'd do this for us?'

That look again and his mouth twisted in a strange smile. 'I'll do it for you,' he said softly and his eyes caressed her. His hand came down again to take hers. 'And now, Dr Gaize, it's time we checked on Paddy and Henry.'

Instead of moving, though, he stood looking down at her. Bonnie's heart twisted in confusion. 'I'd do it for you. . .' The words themselves were a caress—a promise of something precious starting to grow.

Somehow she managed to tear her eyes away. She had to get a grip on herself.

'I. . .yes. . . My uncle will be pleased to see you. . .' She looked across to the house and drew in her breath in horror.

Paddy was walking slowly, falteringly, out the back door. As Bonnie watched in concern he took two stumbling steps forward and crumpled where he stood.

## CHAPTER FOUR

WEBB reached him before Bonnie. He had turned at Bonnie's swift intake of breath, had seen and was running across the yard before Bonnie could make a move. By the time she reached Paddy, Webb was already bending over the Irishman, moving him into recovery position.

'I'll get the oxygen,' Bonnie gasped and kept running through the house to snatch up the portable cylinder and mask. Her uncle was staring up in wide-eyed concern but Bonnie had no time for reassurance. She was back with Paddy in seconds, fitting the mask to the cylinder almost before Webb's hand could reach out for it.

'OK.' The mask was clamped firmly over Paddy's mouth and nose, and Webb shifted to support the man's shoulders. Already Paddy's skin was a sickly, cyanosed blue white. 'Take your time, Paddy.' He spoke loudly and firmly to the almost unconscious man. 'There's no rush to get air in. The oxygen you're breathing will take its effect in a minute. Just lie back and relax. Try to slow down your breathing rate.'

There was dead silence except for the harsh rasping breaths, seemingly torn from Paddy's lungs. Bonnie sank down beside him and took his hand in hers.

'It's OK, Paddy,' she said softly. 'You've just walked longer than you've walked since you broke your leg. It's no wonder your lungs are complaining.'

There was nothing else to do but wait. The sun shone hot on the trio, and the silence accentuated Paddy's desperate fight for breath. A lone chook peered out from under a bush, came closer to investigate and then moved off with a disgusted cluck. Humans usually meant food but even a chook could see this lot had other things on their minds.

Finally the awful fighting eased. Faint colour crept back under Paddy's leathery skin and he put a hand up to push the mask away.

'Not yet, Paddy,' Bonnie told him gently, holding the mask in place. 'Let's get you back to bed first.'

'You can't lift me. . .' It was a supreme effort to say the words and Bonnie grinned down at him.

'I'm a farm girl, born and bred,' she smiled. 'With Dr Halford's help I can lift anything.' Then her smile deepened. 'Besides, if I can't we always have the trailer and the winch. If you weigh as much as the cow we might have to resort to that.'

She looked up to Webb, signalling with her eyes that she was ready to lift. They had to move fast. For the time they were carrying him, there was no oxygen at the end of Paddy's mask.

Webb's eyes were expressionless. He looked like a man who had just been hit by a sledgehammer and had no idea where the hammer had come from or where it was likely to hit again.

'Ready, Dr Halford?' Bonnie's voice held a trace of impatience and Webb recovered.

'Are you sure you can lift?'

'Of course I'm sure,' Bonnie snapped.

Webb shrugged and moved. In seconds the oxygen cylinder was laid aside and he proceeded to partner Bonnie in a fireman's life.

It was a fairly uneven lift. Bonnie was tiny but, as she'd told Paddy, she was strong. Webb took as much of the weight as he could—if Paddy had been less than six feet two and strongly built he could probably have carried him on his own—but even so the weight made

Bonnie stifle a gasp. She managed, though, and in moments Paddy was being laid on his bed. As he was lowered onto the mattress, Bonnie left Webb moving him into position and raced to retrieve the precious oxygen.

It took another five minutes to get Paddy to the point where he could speak and the worry creases around Bonnie's eyes could afford to relax.

All that time Henry hadn't spoken. He had lain helpless in the other bed and stared in increasing concern at what was going on. In a hospital ward Bonnie could have pulled curtains around the bed but there was no such luxury here. Finally, as Paddy's breathing eased to almost normal and Bonnie stepped back from the bed, Henry found his voice.

'He's. . . He's going to be alright. . .'

'He's going to be alright.' Bonnie turned to her uncle and gave him a rather shaky grin. She was trying hard to make her voice reassuring but she was still fighting for breath herself. 'It must have been that church service, I reckon. It brought the gods down on our side.'

Henry gave a shaky chuckle and Bonnie's eyes widened. She hadn't heard Henry laugh since. . .

Since when? She couldn't remember.

'I couldn't have faced it if he'd died,' Henry whispered. 'He went out because of me——'

'I went out because of us,' Paddy retorted from the next bed, his words a breathless whisper. He gasped and retired back to his mask.

'We had visions of you sitting down on the track trying to work up enough courage to shoot the cow,' Henry finished for him. 'And the gun didn't go off—and we waited and waited and then we couldn't bear it any longer and Paddy said he'd do it himself. . .'

'So he came to help.' Bonnie's eyes filled with tears and she turned to take Paddy's hand in hers. 'I might have known. And all the time Dr Halford and I have been saving the little cow's life.'

'Saving. . .' Henry stared from Bonnie's mud-stained face to Webb's and his eyes stayed on Webb. 'Don't tell me you put the leg back in?'

'We did.' Webb's smile was permanently in place now, and his face seemed light years younger than Bonnie had seen it before. He grinned down at Henry like a schoolboy who'd just won a five-pound box of chocolates. 'Me and Dr Gaize. . . I reckon we're capable of anything, don't you, Dr Gaize?'

Henry stared from one to the other. His eyes widened.

'Bloody hell. . .' he whispered.

Webb performed a cursory inspection of both men and left soon after.

'They're fine,' he told Bonnie. 'You're doing a great job.'

'Even if my patients do get out of bed and come looking for me—risking their lives. . .' Bonnie grimaced as she walked back out to Webb's car with him. If they hadn't seen Paddy collapse—— Well, it didn't bear thinking about if he'd lain on the path without help.

'It's my guess that'll do him nothing but good,' Webb reassured her. He reached his car and leaned against it, looking down at his battle-stained colleague. 'If what you say is right and he hasn't tried to get moving at all since he broke his leg, then that might have been just the impetus he needed to get going. If he thinks you need him——'

'You mean I should cry for help twice a day?'

'From small distances,' Webb smiled, his eyes doing strange things to Bonnie's insides. 'Desperately need his help from the other side of the bedroom, then from just outside the door. . . By next week I reckon you might even be able to call for help from the dairy.'

'I hope so,' Bonnie whispered. She made herself meet those eyes. 'I. . . Thank you,' she faltered. 'I can't say how grateful I am.'

'You haven't received my bill yet,' he smiled. 'It's coming.'

Bonnie bit her lip. 'I'll pay.'

'Oh, you'll pay alright,' Webb said softly. He touched her chin lightly with his hand, and his smile faded. 'It seems you owe a debt, Bonnie Gaize, but I've a feeling—a hope, if you like—that you're about to pay your debt in full.'

Bonnie watched the big car make its way slowly back along the farm track. Webb had work to do in town. The medical demands of Kurrara would be enormous, Bonnie knew, and Webb had just given her almost a full morning's work.

She'd have to pay somehow.

Bonnie walked over to the house paddock and gazed at her recovering cow. She'd risen to unsteady legs and, as Bonnie watched, she took a couple of faltering steps forward. The leg was sore—she limped heavily as Bonnie watched—but it bore her weight.

'If he hadn't come you'd be dead by now,' Bonnie told the cow and smiled as the cow cast her a baleful look and applied herself to the ample feed in the paddock. The cow, it seemed, wasn't about to launch into long speeches of gratitude.

'Well, I'm grateful, even if you're not,' Bonnie told the cow's backside. 'So just keep getting better.'

Lunch—— She hadn't even thought about lunch!

Bonnie detoured by the hen house and had another fast search for the missing Frankie, but finally gave up. She must have been taken by a fox. Meanwhile, there was a meal to cook, washing to do, massages, changes of beds, the odd—very odd—spot of housework and then more milking.

'Give me a busy night at Casualty any time,' Bonnie groaned as she made her way back to the house. She was starting to think she would never make the distance.

No more dramas occurred to mar her afternoon, which was just as well, considering her schedule. By the time Bonnie had finished evening milking and had settled her patients she was exhausted. Nine o'clock. Soon she could fall into bed—but first she had to check on her bovine invalid.

By torchlight the little cow was still peacefully grazing. Bonnie milked her dry, scattered some fresh hay around her, and then, while she watched, the cow settled down with an audible grunt of relief. It was a warm night and the little cow would be dry and secure. In a week she'd be recovered enough to rejoin the herd.

So—at least one happy ending. Bonnie turned gratefully towards her bed and then paused as headlights pierced the night. A car was turning into the house track.

Now what?

She stood, torch in hand, waiting for the car to come to a halt. Beside her the two farm dogs came in closer, the hairs on their backs prickling, and Bonnie was grateful for their presence. This was an isolated farmhouse and her two men were hardly any protection.

She recognised the car as it drew to a halt, but only after staring hard. The car was half-camouflaged by a gigantic pine tree, tied haphazardly to the roof rack.

Webb. . .

Bonnie gaped. The lights of the car died with the motor and Webb Halford emerged. He'd seen her torch and looked straight across to where she was standing. In the moonlight she looked absurdly young and defenceless—and unsure.

'Merry Christmas,' he told her, his mouth twisting into a grin. 'Aren't you going to welcome Santa Claus?'

'You don't. . . You don't look like any Santa Claus I've ever known,' Bonnie said breathlessly and Webb Halford laughed. This man was a world away from the contemptuous stranger who had accused her of neglecting her uncle.

'Give me time, girl. When my hair grows white I'll grow whiskers to match. Now, where do you want me to put this?'

'This?'

'In case you hadn't noticed,' he said patiently, 'there is a tree attached to the top of my car. Maybe you thought it was some sort of fancy radio antenna, but I assure you it's a yuletide tree—house, for the decorating thereof.'

'I don't. . .I don't have any decorations.'

'I had noticed that.'

He was talking to her as if she was slightly stupid and Bonnie didn't help at all by spreading her hands in confusion.

'But we don't have anything to put on a tree. My aunt didn't believe in tinsel and things.'

He sighed. 'A man has to think of everything. Do you know how helpless you sound, Dr Gaize?'

Bonnie fought for a grip on herself. 'No. I. . .'

'You sound about ten.' The ropes were unfastened and the tree slid downward. Webb stood surrounded by pine tree, a weird, camouflaged figure in the night.

'It occurred to me today that what you had out here was a hospital of sorts, albeit a fairly bleak one,' he told her. 'This place seems to be lacking a solitary shred of yuletide adornment and what Kurrara hospital has in abundance at the moment is adornment. Every service club in the district has been plying us with decorations, to the point where we have two trees a ward. So——' he reached back and retrieved a box from the passenger seat of his car '—fairy lights, tinsel, balls of glitter—I believe Sister even packed an angel for the top. All you have to say is where you want the thing. And carry the box.'

And carry it quickly. Things were getting away from him. Webb had released the tree to pick up the box, and now the tree was not staying where it had been put.

Webb grimaced, grabbing for the tree but it was too late. The tree swayed perilously and toppled forward. Bonnie lunged to grab it at the same time as Webb dropped his box and lunged as well. Their hands met as the tree toppled and they ended up on the ground, surrounded by pine tree and their eyes inches apart.

There was dead silence. Nothing. The only thing that Bonnie was aware of was the feel of Webb's fingers on hers and the sweet fragrance of pine. The night was like an embrace in itself, enfolding them in warmth and darkness.

'Well, well. . .' Webb eyes were still dangerously laughing in the soft moonlight. His hand released the tree and came up to cup her chin. 'I had thought I'd have to find mistletoe first, but if you insist on throwing yourself into my arms regardless. . .' His other hand came around her shoulders and his mouth dropped to hers.

It was a kiss of warmth and laughter. A kiss meant in the spirit of the season—nothing more, Bonnie told herself desperately as her lips responded to his.

Respond they did, though. It should have been a light, feather kiss of friendship, and yet. . .and yet the feel of his hands on her—the touch of his mouth—the smell of him. . .

Dear heaven—this was no kiss of friendship. His mouth had changed—no longer brushing her lips but seeking, demanding, possessing. . . The laughter had gone and there was only the warmth—the closeness and the desire. . .

Heaven knew what would have been the outcome if it hadn't been for the dogs. The two animals were confused. They knew Bonnie now as their surrogate mistress—the lady in charge of the dinner bowl—and here she was sprawled on the ground with a stranger. No self-respecting dog would tolerate such behaviour and they voiced their indignation as one. They didn't quite attack Webb but their barking drowned out the stillness of the night and one of them lunged forward in an uncertain gesture of defence.

'Down. . .' Webb pulled away and growled effectively at the dog nearest him. Dougal put his tail between his legs and crept forward in an abject gesture of apology and Bonnie gave a shaky laugh.

'Useless dogs,' she managed. 'Can't you see I'm being attacked?'

'Ravished.' Webb's white teeth gleamed in laughter. He rose and then pulled her up to stand beside him. 'Obviously they're trained to prevent attack but not ravishment. Well done, Dr Gaize. . .'

'I didn't train them.' Bonnie's face was bright crimson. She pulled her hand away and made an ineffectual gesture of smoothing down her disreputable jeans. 'Look, thank you for the Christmas tree. You can leave it here and I'll fix it in the morning.'

'It'll be wilting by morning,' Webb told her. 'It needs to be in water now. And I've even brought a stand with its own water container. Just show me where you want it, Dr Gaize, and we'll set it up.'

'It'd be better in the room with Paddy and Henry.' Bonnie was flustered past belief and she was having trouble making her voice work. 'But they'll be asleep—or they should be.'

'They have all day tomorrow to sleep,' Webb told her firmly. 'Half their luck. But tomorrow—tomorrow you and I have the work of the world back on our shoulders. Monday. . . So—let's get this tree up now.'

In the end it was a silly, happy night for all of them. As Bonnie had half-expected, neither of her two patients were asleep, and as Webb carried the tree into the house Henry called out to demand what was happening. His frustration at being confined to bed was plain. Webb carried the tree through into their room, switched on the light and proceeded to include the two of them in a massive decorating plan.

Bonnie was left to watch. Webb insisted it was his tree, and he was in charge, so Bonnie perched on Paddy's bed as spectator as Webb produced tinsel, baubles, angels, fairy lights—everything they could possibly need to transform the room for Christmas.

The tree was vast—almost too big for the room. The wings of the angel brushed the ceiling and Webb worked balanced on a chair.

'If you fall I'll just pull another bed in and have three patients,' Bonnie warned and Webb grinned down at her.

'With you as my doctor the temptation's almost irresistible,' he teased.

'I'm big on enemas,' Bonnie told him severely, and watched as her two elderly men hooted with laughter.

'Don't you believe it, Doc. She's never touched us with one of them murderous medications yet—and she does a great massage.'

'Does she?' Webb's eyes left his angel and moved down to Bonnie, wickedly teasing. 'Well, well. . .'

'Your lights are slipping,' Paddy advised him kindly. 'We know our Dr Gaize is a better sight than any

Christmas tree, but I'd watch the job if I were you.'

'Paddy!' Bonnie's face burned but Webb only laughed and shifted his lights obligingly.

'Is that OK, Henry?' he demanded and Henry considered.

'A bit to the left, I reckon.'

'Sure?'

The transformation in Henry was amazing. He was lit up almost as much as the fairy lights—his face wreathed in laughter. Between the three men, there was a constant stream of jokes and banter.

Paddy and Henry—they were different men, Bonnie thought and her eyes moved back to Webb. For this she had to be grateful to Webb. This was a brilliant idea, and she couldn't have possibly done it herself. To get time to go into town and choose all these things—well, Christmas had come to the farm it seemed, courtesy of Webb Halford.

Webb obligingly moved every ornament until both Henry and Paddy declared themselves content. Finally he delved down to the bottom of his huge cardboard box and produced his final offering—two small twigs of mistletoe. Without a word he walked to each bed in turn and hung the sprig over the bed lights.

'Now, if any likely lady comes into orbit you can try it out,' he grinned. He gestured to Paddy. 'Want to see if it works?'

'My oath I do,' Paddy grinned. He scratched the fabric on the top of his pyjamas. 'Dr Gaize, I've an itch right here,' he whinged. 'Can you have a look?'

Bonnie shrugged, matching Paddy's grin. 'Conniving males. . .'

'I'm not joking.' Paddy was at his most aggrieved. 'It could be fatal if you don't look right now.'

'Oh, yes?' Twinkling with laughter, Bonnie

obligingly walked forward to look, and was grasped by both shoulders and solidly kissed.

'You fraud!' She shook herself free, bubbling with laughter. 'How can you kiss like that and declare you're dying of lung disease? Casanova could hardly pack more punch than you.'

Paddy gave a delighted hoot but Webb had taken Bonnie and steered her over to the other bed.

'I reckon your uncle has a similar problem, if you care to look,' he said.

The laughter died from Bonnie's face. She looked down at Henry and there too, the smile had faded. He seemed almost shrunken onto the pillows.

'How about it, Uncle Henry?' Bonnie asked softly, her heart going out to this sad, defeated man. Somehow Aunt Lois had manipulated Henry into being a person he was afraid to face—and the ghost of Lois seemed all around them.

'Don't be stupid, Henry,' Lois would have said. 'You don't have to kiss the ungrateful brat. It's emotional codswallop. If you must kiss someone then kiss Jacinta—not that she'd want to kiss you when you haven't shaved for twenty-four hours and you haven't changed your shirt. . .'

'Aunt Lois wouldn't approve of this room, would she, Uncle Henry?' Bonnie asked slowly, and watched as the shrinking ceased. Henry's eyes flew to hers—and they seemed almost pleading.

'I think I might claim my kiss, even if you don't want it,' she continued. 'Just because. . .because Aunt Lois isn't here to ridicule me. And this room—well, this room and this Christmas is for you and me. For the past as well as the future.'

'After what we did to you. . .' Henry whispered and Bonnie reached down to take his hand.

'It doesn't matter any more.'

'It does.'

Bonnie shook her head. 'Believe me, it doesn't.' Then she smiled. 'But I would like my mistletoe kiss—if I may.'

The whole room seemingly held its breath. Even Paddy sensed that there were undercurrents here he didn't have a hope of understanding—but now wasn't the time for joking.

And finally, finally, Henry's fingers moved so it wasn't Bonnie who was doing the holding. Her fingers were gripped tight, and he pulled her down to him. Dry lips brushed—oh, so softly—against her forehead and she was released without a word. Bonnie stepped back, but their eyes still held and behind Henry's eyes there was the beginning of light.

'You're right, girl,' he whispered huskily. 'Your aunt would have hated this room. And me—— Me, I love it!'

'So what was that all about?'

Webb walked out to the car with Bonnie beside him. She had wanted to stay in the house, but it seemed churlish not to see him off after all he'd done.

'You mean. . . You mean with my uncle?'

'With your uncle.' Webb stopped by the car and turned to look down at her. 'What else could I mean? The tension between you two can be cut with a knife—and he's almost ashamed to face you.'

Bonnie shrugged. 'We're working it out.'

'So I noticed.' Webb's hands came up to grip her shoulders. 'I had it wrong all round, didn't I? It was your family that did the rejecting, not you.'

'It doesn't matter.'

'I think it does.' His grip tightened. 'Want to tell me about it?'

'No.'

'Your aunt and uncle—did they treat Jacinta the same way? Is that why she also doesn't come near her father?'

'I don't know why Jacinta doesn't come home,' Bonnie said bleakly. 'I haven't spoken to her for years.'

'Real happy families!'

'As you say.' Bonnie had had enough. Weariness was washing through her in waves and the emotional tension was making her feel dizzy. If only he wasn't standing so darned close. . .

'Is it OK to say that I'm sorry?' Webb asked gently, his eyes holding hers in the dim light. 'That I'm sorry for prejudging you?'

'You can apologise?' Bonnie's voice cracked a little. The sympathy and understanding in his voice pierced her with something that was close to anguish. 'Without knowing what really happened?'

'I still don't know the facts.' Webb's hands tightened on her shoulders. 'But I'm starting to know you, and maybe that's enough. Maybe that's enough for any man.'

Bonnie gasped. The tenderness behind the words was all around her—an embrace in itself. She looked wonderingly up to him and, once more, his face came down to hers and she was kissed.

This was like nothing she had ever felt before. Once. . . Once Craig had kissed her and told her he loved her but even then it hadn't felt like this. This was a feeling of drowning and wanting to drown—of tenderness and warmth and passion—and something deep within that she didn't have a name for. Bonnie opened her lips and let the kiss deepen, savouring the warmth of the night and the sensation of feeling herself cherished.

Cherished. . .

The word echoed round and round her head,

seductive in its sweetness, and it was all Bonnie could do to make her traitorous mind think.

What was she doing? Bonnie Gaize—to be surrendering herself to this man without a whimper. She had made a vow. . . Was the first attractive man to kiss her enough to let her break it—to open herself again to heartbreak and loneliness?

Somehow her hands came up to his hard, muscular chest and she pushed, shoving herself backward away from him. Surprised, Webb released her and Bonnie took three fast steps backward.

'N. . . No,' she managed, her voice wobbling dangerously.

Webb didn't move. He stood against the car, looking impossibly handsome in the dim light. His eyes held hers and they were a caress without a touch.

'I don't think you mean that, Bonnie Gaize.'

Bonnie took a deep breath. 'Yes.' Her voice trailed to a whisper. Involuntarily her fingers moved to her lips where she could still feel the pressure of his mouth. 'I do. Please. . .I don't want you to touch me.'

'That's not what it felt like.'

'I don't care!' She shook her head, her curls swinging against her cheeks. 'It's what I want.'

'You've taken a vow of chastity?' He sounded bemused more than anything and Bonnie felt a faint stirring of anger. He was so darned arrogant. He thought he just had to kiss her and she'd swoon at his feet. Well, she had no intention of swooning—no matter what her tremulous heart was doing within her breast.

'That's right,' she said grimly. 'I don't need a man, Dr Halford. Now, or ever.'

'I didn't say you did.' He stepped forward but Bonnie just as fast stepped backward again and Webb gave up the attempt. Once more he leaned back against the car and there was a smile lurking in the twist of his mouth and the gleam in his dark eyes. 'You're a lady who doesn't need a family. A lady with career intentions. Which I'd like to know, incidentally. Where are you going in your medical career?'

The question threw her even more off-balance than she already was. Bonnie faltered and then recovered.

'I'm starting my physician training,' she told him. 'I start work on my first part in March.'

'Well, bully for you.'

'There's no need to mock me.'

'I'm not mocking you,' Webb told her, the laughter fading from his voice. 'I'd never mock you—not now.'

'No?'

'No, Bonnie. I wouldn't.'

'Well, if you don't intend to mock me——' Bonnie took a deep breath and swallowed '—perhaps you'll also take me seriously when I say I'm not in the market for an affair. I don't need or want a man in my life in any way, shape or form.'

'You have two inside the house,' Webb said mildly. 'Two very dependent males, I'd say.'

'That's different,' Bonnie snapped and she heard the laughter come back into Webb's voice.

'I'd certainly hope so.'

'Look. . .' Bonnie spread her hands a trifle desperately. Things were out of her control and she didn't like it one bit. 'Please, Dr Halford, I'm dead tired. It's near eleven and I have to be up early for milking. If there's nothing else you need to say then I'll say goodnight.'

'How's our cow?' The laughter was still there.

'She's fine. She's up.'

'So I have three patients to look in on tomorrow.'

'There's not the slightest need for you to look

in,' Bonnie snapped. 'I'm managing fine on my own—just fine.'

'And that's just the problem,' Webb said ruefully, pulling open the car door. He lowered himself into the driver's seat and flashed her a last, long look. 'I'm not sure I want you to any more.'

It took ten minutes before Bonnie's colour had subsided enough for her to return to the house. The fairy lights were still blazing from the men's room as Bonnie walked in. Both men were watching for her, eyes bright with expectant curiosity.

'Kissed you good and proper, did he?' Paddy asked and chuckled as Bonnie's face flamed again. 'Good lad! I wish I was half my age and I'd be tempted to give him a run for his money.'

'Paddy. . .'

'It'll be diamonds next,' Paddy told Henry. 'You mark my words.'

'No. . .' Henry was watching his niece through worried eyes. 'I don't think. . .I don't think you ought to let him kiss you, Bonnie.'

'Well, neither do I, Uncle Henry,' Bonnie told him, moving to plump his pillows and help him shift position in the bed. 'I don't know what the two of you are talking about.'

'Oh, I know what we're talking about.' There was still worry in Henry's voice and, as she turned him, his hand came to grip hers. 'Bonnie, girl, don't. . .'

She paused. There was real fear in Henry's voice.

'Don't what?' She smiled down at Henry's worried face. 'Don't fall for Webb Halford's good looks? You have no need to tell me that, Uncle Henry. Once is enough.'

They both grimaced, and the threadbare memories of Craig drifted back into both their minds.

'I'm glad of that,' Henry muttered. He winced as

he tried to shift himself on his painful hip. 'It's just. . .'

'Just what?'

'Well, you know Webb Halford is married?'

## CHAPTER FIVE

MARRIED. . .

The cheat! Bonnie lay wakeful until the small hours of the morning and let her new knowledge drift around and around her troubled mind.

'Do you know that for sure?' she'd asked incredulously and Henry had nodded.

'He and his wife live up behind the hospital with their little boy. I don't listen to gossip much so I don't know what goes on, but I've seen the three of them around town together plenty of times. The little one looks a bit of a scamp—nice little tacker, but skinny! Like his mum. Serena Halford doesn't seem to fit in here—wears real trendy overall things, like you see in magazines. Platinum blonde but it doesn't seem like it comes from a bottle. She's a real looker!'

'Better than our Bonnie?' Paddy had demanded and Henry had shaken his head.

'Doesn't matter, does it? She's the one he married.' He had looked up at Bonnie and seen anger welling in her face. 'I thought. . .' He had grimaced unhappily. 'I just thought I ought to say something now. It seemed. . .it seemed almost as if he fancied you—and if he kissed you. . .'

'Well, you're right about that,' Bonnie had told him savagely. 'I'm glad you told me.' She had stared from Henry to Paddy and back again, warmth and fun fading from her as if they'd never been. Men!

'All men are toads!' she had finally muttered.

Paddy and Henry had tried to laugh at her anger, but even their light-hearted banter couldn't cheer her.

Bonnie slid into bed feeling sick with depression.

It didn't ease. Bonnie would have said that she didn't have time to think of Webb Halford, but to her disgust he refused to be banished from her thoughts.

It wouldn't be so hard if the man stayed away. She spent the following morning resolutely prohibiting every trace of Webb Halford from entering her thoughts, but as she finished making the beds the big grey car nosed into the driveway and she was right back where she started.

Somehow she managed to be cordially formal, hiding her anger under a blanket of professional rigidity. To her fury it seemed Webb was more amused than anything.

'The way we're going we'll have Paddy dancing an Irish jig for Christmas,' he told her, ignoring her set face and concentrating on Paddy's chest. 'OK, Paddy, let's see you walk across the room.'

Paddy looked uncertainly at Bonnie.

'Paddy's my patient,' Bonnie muttered. 'I should say——'

'When he'll get up.' Webb finished the sentence for her and raised his eyebrows in sardonic amusement. 'So you should. So say it, Dr Gaize.'

'We'll do it this afternoon.'

'I've fifteen minutes free now,' Webb told her. 'I'm due in morning surgery at ten—and I don't think Paddy should be practising his walking skills with just a runt of a doctor like you to support him when he falls.'

'A runt!'

'A runt,' he repeated and then flicked another glance at his watch. 'OK, Paddy, let's move. Let's make two laps of the veranda before I have to go.'

To Paddy's delight he made it practically unaided, falling back into bed exhausted at the end but not having to take recourse to oxygen.

'You know, your plans about dying in the next few weeks are going to have to be altered,' Webb said severely. 'If you've booked the undertaker, I'd telephone and put him on hold for a few months. Or years.'

Bonnie smiled reluctantly. Things were certainly going well for Paddy—this morning he'd eaten a mammoth breakfast and was improving almost as she watched.

There was no answering smile on Paddy's face. His eyes appeared to dull. There seemed little joy in the prospect of living for Paddy.

Like Bonnie, Webb saw the change in Paddy's face.

'The undertaker has some appeal then?' he asked gently and Bonnie held her breath.

'Yeah, well. . .'

'Well, what?'

Paddy shrugged. 'I'm booked into a nursing home. The social worker at the hospital booked me in and gave me a brochure.' He leaned over to his bedside table and shoved it at Webb. 'Does this seem the sort of place you'd like to spend your declining years?'

Webb picked up the brochure and read it thoughtfully before placing it aside. 'You were a farmer?'

'Too right I was.'

'Then you shouldn't go to a nursing home like this,' he agreed. 'It's city based with a city orientation. I can do better than that.'

'Yeah?'

'I can.' Webb smiled down at Paddy's look of patent disbelief. 'We have a hostel and nursing home in Kurrara—out the back of the hospital. Because its residents are mostly farmers we've orientated the place towards farming. It looks out over miles and miles of paddock—the place has its own house cow and we run a small farmlet operated by the residents. It sounds more your cup of tea than this place.'

It certainly did. Bonnie bit back her fury at Webb Halford and managed to smile. 'When you're up and moving we'll go and see it,' she told Paddy. 'That is. . .' She looked uncertainly at Webb. 'How long's the waiting list?'

'For ambulatory patients it's not long at all,' Webb told her and then looked down at Paddy. 'So it's up to you. Ambulate!'

'Ambulate?'

'Get on your feet and walk. As much as you can.'

'And when are you going to say the same thing to me?' Henry asked wistfully from the other bed and Webb shook his head.

'Two weeks more,' he told him. 'You play somersaults with tractors, then you expect repercussions. Those bones have to heal before you move.' He looked around at the big French windows opening onto the veranda and then down at Henry's bed. 'Tell you what. I have some castor cups at the hospital. If I brought them out then your bed could be wheeled out to the veranda and you could supervise while Paddy practises his ambulation. If you like I'll see if I can find a long stock whip so you can nudge him along when he slows down.'

Henry grinned and nodded as Paddy squeaked a protest. 'I'd like that.'

'Fine. I'll bring them out this evening.'

Henry flashed an uncertain look up at his niece's face. He saw the dismay, quickly hidden.

'It seems to me that you're neglecting your family, young man,' he said at last. 'Spending time out here.'

Webb smiled and shook his head. 'Serena and Sam are in Melbourne Christmas shopping for the week,' he smiled. 'They tell me it's my duty to stay here and earn money so they can spend more.' He spread his hands. 'So——' he laughed down at Bonnie '—this week I'm almost free—barring the demands of three thousand-odd patients.'

Almost free. . . It was all Bonnie could do not to walk over and slap his arrogant face. He stood laughing down at her, and Bonnie felt the old familiar lurch of rejection in the pit of her stomach.

Love wasn't for the likes of Bonnie Gaize. Once she vaguely remembered her parents loving her, but they'd left her with her aunt and uncle while they'd gone overseas—and they'd never returned. A car crash in Italy. It wasn't until Bonnie was in her teens that she'd started asking herself why Bonnie wasn't in the back seat with them. They only had one little girl—surely it wouldn't have been too much trouble to take Bonnie with them—or hadn't they wanted her? The conclusion was obvious.

And Aunt Lois hadn't wanted her, that was for sure. She'd done her duty in a thoroughly nasty and vitriolic manner—and Bonnie had learned early how displays of affection were met. She'd learned to hide her need.

And then—half-way through medical school she'd met Craig and she'd stupidly, stupidly given her heart—only to have her love thrown back at her as something worthless and laughable. Laughable. That was what love was—and here was Webb Halford laughing down at her and her heart was feeling so empty and cold she wished for the thousandth time that she didn't have one. How to stop falling for people—how to stop loving. . .

She didn't love Webb Halford. She didn't. This cold, sick feeling was something she'd hoped never to feel again and she just had to get rid of it as soon as possible. She clenched her nails into her palms and strove for professional calm.

'Uncle Henry tells me there's a physiotherapist comes to the hospital twice a week,' she managed. 'Is it possible to arrange a house visit here?'

'I can do that.' Webb looked at her strangely, aware of the tension in her voice. 'It'd help Paddy too. That chest could do with some work. Maggie, the physio, doesn't usually do house calls but seeing we've two patients here, I'll talk her into it.'

I bet you will, Bonnie thought savagely. Especially if she's young and attractive. You could charm blood out of stone, Webb Halford.

'Is anything wrong, Dr Gaize?'

'No.' She met his look, her eyes cold and repelling. 'If that's all, I have work to do, Dr Halford.'

'So I'm dismissed?'

'If you like.' She was being rude but she didn't care. She walked to the door and held it wide. 'Thank you for coming. I'm sure Henry appreciates your visits.'

'But you don't?' He crossed to where she stood and frowned down at her.

'Not especially. I've told you before, I can manage.'

'I'm sure you can. I'm sure if I hadn't come you would have put the cow's leg back in—and you would have brought home an even larger Christmas tree in your tiny sports car. It might have looked amazing though—travelling along the highway. Forest on wheels!'

It didn't raise a smile. Her eyes stayed cold.

'I know,' she muttered. 'I'm grateful. But please. . . Unless I contact you there's no need to come again.'

'I think there is.'

'Well, I don't.' Bonnie looked appealingly over at her uncle. 'You don't want Dr Halford to keep coming, do you, Uncle?'

Henry looked from Bonnie to Webb and then back again. He sighed, seeing the tension on Bonnie's face. He could do this much at least for the girl.

'No,' he said firmly. 'We can manage without him.'

There was a long, long silence. Webb looked at the three of them, and each face was set. Finally he nodded.

'Well, then. I accept your lack of hospitality and my professional dismissal. I'm going past the farm tonight as I have an elderly lady out this way I promised to drop in on. I'll put the castor cups in the mail box as I pass.' He lifted a hand and touched Bonnie's face, then frowned as she winced. 'Will you walk me out to the car, Dr Gaize?'

'No.'

He nodded again, as though he had expected as much. 'Let me know if you need me,' he said bluntly and walked out the door.

So that was that.

Bonnie performed the rest of her morning chores in a dreary stupor. Webb Halford was dismissed and she needn't see him again. She probably wouldn't have seen him much anyway, even if she hadn't been so bluntly dismissive. Once his wife and child were back in town he'd have little time for turning the heads of stupid young females who should know better.

If only she could stop feeling that kiss! If only it didn't stay with her every waking minute, demanding a response from her aching heart.

Drat the man! She had work to do—so she should just get on and do it.

She didn't see Webb Halford for three days.

That evening she walked down the track to the farm gate to find four cup castors in the mail box and a walking frame leaning against the gate. Webb had taken her at her word and not come near.

She should be glad. She should. . .

Heaven, there was enough to do without thinking of Webb. Now that Paddy had decided to live, her work-load was increased, bullying him back and forth across the veranda, assisting him into the shower and generally mobilising him again. The walking frame was invaluable as it gave support to Paddy and he wasn't dependent on Bonnie's slight body when he faltered.

With the help of the castors, she moved Henry's bed onto the veranda during the day. From his new vantage point, Henry gently encouraged Paddy on—and Bonnie couldn't but marvel at Henry's increased communication. He was making an effort to speak—something he hadn't done in the whole time Bonnie had known him. Between Paddy and Henry a gentle camaraderie was growing, taking the form of quiet ribbing and laughter bubbling just beneath the surface.

The radio was almost constantly on—blaring Christmas carols around the farm in relentless celebration of the season. The intercom took the carols to Bonnie wherever she went.

Four more shopping days until Christmas, the radio prodded, and Bonnie winced. She'd bought her Christmas present to herself. Her little red car sat in the yard, looking slightly silly. A couple of chooks had perched on its soft top and left their mark, and there was mud spattered along the side. Her salesman would cringe if he could see it now.

Still. . . For some odd reason the car continued to give her pleasure. She walked past it every time she went to the dairy and as she passed she invariably ran her hand along its gleaming paintwork.

I can be independent, she told herself. I can have fun. Even if I never get to England I can buy myself silly, indulgent whims that give me pleasure—and I don't need to be dependent on other people to get that pleasure.

I don't need to be dependent on Webb Halford.

For heaven's sake. . .

Why did she have to say that to herself? There had

never been any suggestion that she become dependent on the man. He'd kissed her twice—two kisses that meant nothing more to him than a mild flirtation while his wife was away. Maybe he'd do the same thing while his wife was here. He wasn't to know that Bonnie couldn't accept his kisses lightly—that somehow his body—his voice—his eyes—had affected her so much that nothing Webb Halford did could be regarded by Bonnie as inconsequential.

'For heaven's sake, stop thinking of Webb Halford and start thinking of Christmas,' Bonnie told herself crossly. 'Order a turkey and champagne—and think about how to make a Christmas pudding this late in the season. You can't give Paddy and Henry a shop-bought pudding.'

She went to bed fiercely forcing her mind to concentrate on such momentous problems as pudding-making, shoving the thought of Webb Halford resolutely to one side. He refused to be shoved, though—and at one in the morning she was still staring at the ceiling, her mind a weird jumble of brandy sauce and dark, piercing eyes.

The harsh jangle of the telephone made her jump a foot.

In this silent farmhouse the sound of its ringing seemed almost an obscenity. Telephones in the middle of the night were for nights in her city hospital—not for here. This telephone had hardly rung in the time she'd been home and Bonnie had only used it herself to order groceries.

She slid swiftly out of bed, padding barefoot fast across the hall to reach it before it woke Paddy and Henry.

Too late, of course. Both men had jerked awake.

'What is it, girl?' Henry's voice was anxious. Telephone calls in the middle of the night were harbingers of disaster until proved otherwise.

'I'll tell you in a minute.' Bonnie lifted the receiver. 'Yes?'

'Bonnie?' Webb Halford's voice snapped down the line and Bonnie knew at once that for whatever reason he'd rung her, his need was urgent. 'Bonnie, I'm sending a nurse out to stay with Paddy and Henry. I need you here.'

'You need. . .' Bonnie took a deep breath, responding to the urgency of his tone. 'Why?' She wasn't protesting. This was a professional need.

'Bill Roberts. Dr Roberts—my partner. He's past seventy and shouldn't be practising at the level he is, but he refuses to quit. One of his patients rang him at home and demanded a house call. Instead of calling me, he went on his own.' A brief silence and Bonnie could sense Webb's eyes, grim and bleak. 'He either fell asleep in front of the wheel or he had a stroke or heart attack. The latter, I'd guess. Anyway, he ran his car straight into the path of an oncoming vehicle. A family coming home from a Christmas party—two adults and three kids. Bill Roberts is dead—even though the cars didn't collide—but the family veered off into a tree, and they're a mess. I need help, Bonnie. Can you come?'

'Yes. How soon will the nurse be here?' Bonnie was wide awake now, personal animosity thrust aside. To be a doctor alone with five badly injured casualties was appalling—and the nearest town wasn't big enough to provide support. The air ambulance would have to come from Melbourne but if patients needed stabilising. . .

'She left two minutes ago.'

'She knows where to come?'

'Yes.' Webb hesitated. 'She's an aide, Bonnie, but she can resuscitate and I need skilled personnel here.'

'That's OK. I'll be in town in ten minutes.'

'Have you done anaesthetics?'

'Two terms.'

'Praise be. See you in Theatre.' The phone was slammed down.

From peace to life-and-death drama in seconds!

Bonnie felt the familiar surge of adrenalin as she told the men what was happening. It wasn't perfect to leave them without a fully qualified nurse, but Webb would have weighed the needs and come to a decision. It was hard, but if the choice was that three children might die or an elderly man might slip away with emphysema there was no real choice—and everyone involved knew it.

Paddy appeared well, though. He'd woken from sound sleep and his breathing seemed secure.

'Go on, girl,' he growled. 'Don't wait for the nurse. Five minutes alone isn't going to kill us—I promise faithfully I'll keep breathing every single second and if Henry doesn't do likewise I'll get up and kick him until he does. So get a move on.'

Bonnie did. Two minutes later she was dressed in clean jeans and blouse. She ran outside, and as she pulled open the door of her sports car the nurse's car pulled into the road gate.

The woman saw Bonnie against the veranda and waved, signalling against her headlights that she'd opened the gate and would wait for Bonnie to go through before closing it. Bonnie didn't hesitate. Her tyres skidded as she did a fast turn out of the yard, slowing fractionally to give a swift greeting to her replacement, and then she headed for town.

The scene in Casualty was the stuff of nightmares. Bonnie walked into the hospital five minutes later and was met by chaos.

Not even ordered chaos. The team here was working without a leader. Webb was nowhere to be seen.

'Dr Halford?' Bonnie snapped, her voice rising above the din. There was a woman hysterically sobbing over a stretcher where a child seemed to be unconscious. A man was groaning from another stretcher—a steady, agonised moan that set teeth on edge—and another child was crying frantically for its mother. One nurse was unsuccessfully trying to soothe the sobbing child while another was trying to reason with the mother.

There was no sense in adding to the noise. Bonnie walked swiftly over to the nurse beside the mother, took her shoulders and swung her round to face her. Stunned, the nurse turned within Bonnie's grasp.

'Where's Dr Halford? I'm Dr Gaize and Dr Halford said he needs me.'

'Oh. . .' The nurse gave a faltering, frightened smile, clearly at a loss. Bonnie didn't look like a doctor—but her voice sure sounded like she was. Bonnie had imbued it with every trace of authority she could muster. 'He's. . . There's a child with a punctured lung. He's in Theatre with her. He wants you in there as soon as you arrive.'

'He's assessed these?' Bonnie glanced around again, her eyes coming to rest on the injured man. Surely Webb wouldn't have left him like this?

'As best he can. Except. . .the man came in later. He had to be cut from the car so Dr Halford hasn't seen him. We can't call him out of Theatre because the child he's with is dying. Her face is crushed and her lung. . .'

'OK.' Bonnie's voice rose again, cutting off the words. It wouldn't help the hysteria for the rest of the family to hear this. She glanced around again, thinking fast. 'Get me some morphine. And a saline drip.' The man was in agony and if he hadn't been assessed then he had to be first priority. 'Now.'

Ignoring the chaos behind her, she did a careful examination of the injured man. It took a certain amount of trust in Webb Halford to ignore the unconscious child—but the nurse said he'd been assessed by Webb and Bonnie had seen enough of Webb Halford to know the child wouldn't be neglected if his life was in danger. Somehow he'd be within reach of Webb Halford.

The woman sobbed on behind them, but Bonnie managed to block it out. It was no favour to the woman to comfort her while leaving her husband possibly dying.

It was the man's legs that needed attention, and Bonnie winced as she saw the extent of the damage. The dashboard must have crushed down into his thighs and one of his legs was buckled above the knee at a horrid angle.

It wasn't the break that worried Bonnie, but its effect. Her fingers felt the cold, blue lower leg, searching for a trace of pulse. Nothing.

'I want morphine, now.' The nurse hadn't moved and Bonnie swung around in annoyance. 'And a drip set up. How long's he been here?' she snapped.

'Ten minutes.'

Another nurse, patently senior to the two already present, appeared by Bonnie's side with a syringe of morphine. Thankfully, Bonnie injected it.

Ten minutes. . . He'd spent much more time than that in the car, she guessed, all the while with an obstruction to the circulation in his leg. . .

'Let it be a kink and not a tear in the femoral artery,' she prayed silently, knowing that if the artery was torn there was little that could be done to save the leg. A vascular surgeon might produce a miracle, but vascular surgeons were thin on the ground in this place. There was only Bonnie and Webb.

Webb. . . What Webb was doing may have to be interrupted if they were to save the leg.

'Let's take him through to X-Ray,' she told the senior nurse. 'I want lateral and antero-posterior pictures.'

'I can do that,' the nurse told her and at Bonnie's amazed look she gave a rueful smile. 'I trained as a radiographer before I came to live in Kurrara, but I trained as a nurse too.'

'Praise be.' There was some joy at least, and it left Bonnie free for a moment. She set up a drip and sent both the senior and junior nurses with the trolley to X-Ray before turning her attention to the mother. OK, Webb needed her, but she needed to see those X-rays before she was caught up somewhere else.

The woman, of all of them, seemed the least hurt. She was crouched over the unconscious child, sobbing desperately on his chest. Bonnie walked across and pulled her back.

'Ma'am?' She cast an appealing look at the remaining nurse who responded.

'It's Mrs Bell.'

'Mrs Bell.' Bonnie's voice firmed. She lifted a stethoscope from a nearby tray, bent over the child and listened. What she heard reassured her. Webb had known what he was doing to list this little one as a low priority. The child's heartbeat was steady and his breathing was deep. She flicked back an eyelid. He was unconscious, but the tiny flickering of pupil suggested that the unconsciousness wouldn't last. A jagged cut on his forehead told its own story.

'Has this little one been X-rayed?'

The nurse nodded. 'We X-rayed both this one and his sister—the child Dr Halford's taken to Theatre.' She spoke in an undervoice, conscious of the woman.

'The little girl is in all sorts of trouble but he can't see any signs of intracranial bleed in Toby.'

Bonnie nodded, her hands gently pushing the woman into a chair beside the stretcher.

'Mrs Bell, I need you.'

The woman looked up, white with fear. 'Toby's dying.'

'Toby's not dying.' Bonnie's voice was more certain than she felt, but she had to make a decision. She was the only doctor and she needed control. 'He's had a bang on the head and it'll take him a while to regain consciousness. Meanwhile he's the only member of your family who doesn't need you.' She took the woman's hand and knelt to look closely at her face. 'Can you help me?'

The woman gulped audibly and choked back tears. 'Y. . . Yes.'

Bonnie nodded. 'Well done,' she said softly. 'I need your strength now. We all do.' There was a nasty graze down the woman's cheek and her nose had bled. Bonnie reached for a swab and cleaned the blood from her face. A minor procedure, maybe the most minor of anything she would do this night, but vital for all that. It made Mrs Bell look almost normal—almost like the mother the children so badly needed to see. If this woman could reassure the rest of the family—if she could find the strength to do it—then the nurses would have much less shock to contend with.

The child in the nurse's care was still sobbing. The sobs themselves reassured Bonnie. If the child was capable of that noise then there wasn't too much wrong.

'She's broken her arm,' the nurse told Bonnie as Bonnie crossed to see.

'OK.' Bonnie lifted the little girl onto her lap, snapped her orders to the nurse, and administered sedative and pain-killer. Then she lifted the little girl and laid her down on a stretcher beside her mother.

The sobs stopped almost instantaneously as the mother reached out to cradle her. Reassured about her unconscious son, the woman had energy to soothe. Bonnie pulled blankets over the pair of them. The arm had to be set but it could wait. It was certainly the least urgent need.

Clustered like this, the family was more difficult to treat—but much less likely to give way to hysteria.

'Put Mr Bell's trolley on the other side of his wife as soon as he's done with X-Ray,' Bonnie ordered, setting up a saline drip over the mother. Shock was taking its toll, and this woman had her work cut out for her over the next few hours—or months. She smiled down at the woman. 'You're doing a terrific job,' she whispered.

'Sophie. . .' the woman muttered. 'My husband. . .'

'Your husband's having his legs X-rayed and will be back in a moment before we taken him to Theatre. He's lost circulation in his foot and we'll have to restore it.'

'And Sophie's in Theatre with Dr Halford, so she's in good hands.' It was the senior nurse speaking. The X-rays finished, the trolley with the injured father was being wheeled out. The nurse signalled Bonnie. 'The X-rays are in there for you to see. I can look after things out here.'

A good nurse was worth her weight in diamonds, Bonnie thought gratefully. She cast another swift glance over her four patients, saw the little boy stir and open fearful eyes, and made her escape.

It was the fastest reading of X-rays she had ever done in her life, but what she saw made her even faster. . . The leg was smashed but not so badly that they might not be able to reposition it. If the bone had been crushed then the chance that the artery was irreparably damaged was high. Now, though. . . There was a good chance they were dealing with a kink. If they could just get him to Theatre fast!

Webb was more than ready for her. Bonnie walked through the theatre doors to find Webb already scrubbed and gowned.

'At last,' he snapped. 'You took your time.'

Bonnie flushed. 'The ambulance brought Mr Bell in,' she replied, trying to keep her voice calm.

'And?'

Bonnie's eyes flew up to Webb's. It wasn't anger behind his voice—it was desperation and strain.

'You know them?'

'Trevor Bell is the local publican,' he told her. 'A personal friend. And this little one——' he motioned down to the child on the operating table '—this is Sophie. She's my son's best friend.'

'Her father will live,' Bonnie said quickly, seeing the worst of his fears written behind his eyes. She spoke softly so the frightened child wouldn't hear. 'His legs are damaged and we have a circulation problem that needs urgent attention.'

'It has to wait.' Webb turned back to Sophie. The child was conscious, writhing in shock and panic, and gagging against a plastic airway. 'We'll have to gas. There's a pneumothorax. The fourth rib's punctured the lung and I need to insert a seal. I can't calm her enough to do it under a local.'

'Her face. . .'

The child's face had been crushed, as though she had been dragged along. . .

'Gravel?' she asked and Webb grimaced.

'No seat belt,' he said grimly. 'She has broken cheek bones and she's bleeding into the back of her throat. But, Bonnie, I have to get a seal into place. She's in respiratory distress—not inflating the left lung.'

Bonnie nodded. The air being released from the punctured lung would be building inside the chest wall. Not only would the punctured lung be inoperative, but the pressure of air could push one lung against the other, hampering the effectiveness of the remaining lung.

They couldn't do a lot while the child was in this state, though. Webb had been trying to prepare the chest for an incision under local, but the child's panic made it impossible.

'Stick with the lung,' Bonnie said softly, her eyes taking in the little girl's panic-stricken eyes. It wasn't pain, it was just plain terror that was making the child fight against the airway. 'Maybe we can do this without a general anaesthetic.'

She moved to the head of the bed and took the child's hand in hers.

'Stop fighting, Sophie,' she said in her best school-marm voice. 'You can hear me. You're making yourself sick. Stop fighting.'

After one hard glance at Bonnie, Webb was already swabbing the chest wall and injecting local anaesthetic, taking Bonnie at her word.

The child choked and gagged, and Bonnie swiftly examined her mouth. A nasty, lateral split in her inner lip was bleeding into her mouth. It was the bleeding that had forced Webb to insert the airway so he could concentrate on the lung. With two doctors, though. . .

'I'm taking out the airway,' she told Webb, her eyes still holding Sophie's. 'Sophie doesn't like it, and with me here checking, we can manage without it.'

Swiftly she sucked the mouth clear, turned Sophie's face slightly to the side so the blood ran in a pool in her cheek rather than straight down her throat, and then she lifted the plastic airway out. Sophie gave a ragged gasp of relief.

'Sophie, there's a cut on your lip that's bleeding,' she told the child, her body blocking effectively the sight of what Webb was doing. 'I'm going to stop it, if that's OK with you. Yes?'

The child gave a frightened wheeze that may or may not have been assent, and Bonnie smiled.

'Good girl. Your mum and dad are outside waiting for you, and as soon as we've settled this bleeding we'll take you to see them.' It was hardly the time to tell her how badly injured her father was. This child needed reassurance first and foremost.

It seemed to work. Sophie lay passive while Bonnie injected local anaesthetic around the lip. Using mosquito forceps, she found the spurting artery, clamped it and then stitched. The bleeding died to nothing.

The child relaxed as Bonnie tied the last stitch. Shock was taking over. Her eyes dulled in near sleep and Bonnie held her hand as she continued the gentle suction of her mouth.

Her body still blocked what Webb was doing, and from Sophie's point of view all she could feel was gentle pressure on her chest. As Sophie drifted towards exhausted sleep, Bonnie turned to watch.

The local anaesthetic had taken effect. Webb had already made an incision—about an inch-and-a-half long—between the fourth and fifth ribs, using artery forceps to break open the layers of muscle. As Bonnie turned, a tiny hiss of escaping air signalled he had reached his target.

With half an eye on Sophie's drowsy face, Bonnie assisted as best she could. She was relieved to see how swiftly Webb's skilled fingers moved as they inserted the slender plastic tubing into the chest cavity. Kurrara was fortunate, she thought, to have this man as its general practitioner.

Its only doctor. The other doctor in the town was dead. The pressures on this man working so intently beside her were now enormous.

Webb was still moving fast, attaching the tube securely in place with tape, and carefully, carefully, sealing the tubing with Sleek. No air must be allowed to enter the cavity through the incision.

Webb had used the time waiting for Bonnie to have the intercostal catheter ready. The tube was now connected to the underwater seal, and the air started bubbling out through the lungs. This way air could escape through the punctured lungs but no fluid or air could finds its way back into the lung from the chest until the wound healed.

'No other injuries?' Bonnie asked as Webb fixed the catheter into position.

'I'm not sure. There's certainly some internal bleeding, but she was semi-conscious when we brought her in and she hasn't lost consciousness. With luck. . .'

That was what they were praying for now, Bonnie thought. Luck.

'We'll have to get her to Melbourne if we don't want that face to scar. She needs plastic surgeons,' Webb said grimly. 'I've already contacted the air ambulance. It's pressurised and can travel low in deference to Sophie's lung. Now—let's see Trevor. . .'

The senior nurse had already prepped Trevor Bell, and as Sophie was wheeled from Theatre, they wheeled Trevor in. His leg was still ice cold and blue, and Webb whistled in dismay as he saw it.

'OK, Trev mate,' he said gently to his semi-conscious friend. 'We've patched up your wife and your kids. They're all going to be fine. What we have to do now is get your toes wriggling.'

Bonnie carefully administered general anaesthetic—there was no way they could manipulate such a break with local—while Webb studied the X-rays. As Trevor slid into oblivion, Webb gently, painstakingly, manoeuvred the shattered limb into a more normal position.

It took time. All the while, the toes stayed ice cold, and Bonnie glanced at their colour with a sinking heart.

Finally, the leg where he wanted it, Webb applied light traction, extending the leg to its straightest. It was all he could do. Hopefully the artery was now straighter, its kink removed. Hopefully. . . They waited, Bonnie and Webb, and it was all Bonnie could do to watch the dials rather than the colour of the toes.

And then there was an almost soundless whistle of relief from Webb.

'Bingo,' he whispered and turned to give Bonnie a jubilant grin. There was no mistake. The faintest trace of pink was seeping back into the lower leg, and Webb's fingers moved fractionally on the ankle.

'We have pulse,' he said in satisfaction. 'We've done the thing, Bonnie Gaize. We've done it!'

At five a.m. the air ambulance landed on the runway beside the hospital, waking every patient with its din.

'It can't be helped,' Webb said wearily. 'We use another airstrip when it's not urgent, but I'm not subjecting this family to one inch of extra journey than I must.' They'd decided to send the entire family. Trevor needed specialist orthopaedic surgeons, Sophie needed plastic surgery and to separate the family would induce more stress.

To their relief there were two doctors on board the plane—both an accident and emergency registrar and an anaesthetist. With three trained nurses, the family were almost in better hands than they'd been in in Kurrara.

'Though you've done a great job,' the A and E doctor told them as he inspected the little girl's chest and face. 'We'll take good care of her. With the set-up on the plane the pressure changes should cause minimal concern. Once we're in Melbourne I'll organise for you to be contacted if anything changes.'

'You do that.' Webb ran his hand through his hair in absolute weariness. 'The whole town will be wanting to know.'

'There was a death,' the other doctor said tentatively. He knew Webb personally, it seemed, and Bonnie guessed this plane made relatively frequent flights to this remote area. 'Doc Roberts. Webb, do you want us to take the body?'

Webb shook his head. 'No. He's. . .he was my partner—and my friend. His wife will want the body to stay here.'

'The police say they'll need a post mortem though, Webb,' the doctor said, his voice softening in understanding as he saw the pain on Webb's face. 'He ran off the road for no reason. With no pathologist here——'

'I can do the post mortem.'

'Not if he was your friend.' The A and E doctor shook his head. 'Unethical, Dr Halford, as well as unwise.'

'He's not going to Melbourne.'

Webb's fish clenched and Bonnie looked wonderingly up at him. Webb was past the limits of pain. The senior partner in his practice had been killed—and his daughter's best friend might still go the same route if there were internal injuries. Sometimes medicine—life—was cruel.

'I'll do the post mortem if it's necessary,' she told them and Webb wheeled to face her.

'You can't.'

Bonnie shrugged. 'I'm as qualified as you, Webb Halford, and considerably less involved.'

'What's your training?' The A and E doctor looked at her curiously but relaxed as she told him.

'That's the best idea then, Webb. Leave it to Dr Gaize and stay right out of it. If you can't find anything or run into trouble let us know and we'll fix transport to the nearest pathologist.' He swung himself up into the plane. 'And don't call me back for a few months. I enjoy a lazy life.'

Webb and Bonnie stood together watching as the plane roared off down the strip. The nurses were already wheeling the trolleys back into the hospital. Drama over—until next time.

Finished. The adrenalin flowed from Bonnie, leaving her limp and weary. How much worse must it be for Webb? She looked up into his exhausted face.

'You did the best you could,' she said gently. Indeed, he'd done so much better than she expected. For a country GP his surgical skills were impressive. He'd operated with a precision many surgeons would envy.

'You're no slouch yourself.' He seemed to be almost echoing her thoughts. 'Thank you, Dr Gaize.'

'I wish I could say it was my pleasure.' Bonnie shrugged and glanced at her watch. She should be starting milking around now. 'Could you. . . Could you organise someone later in the morning to relieve me so I can perform the post mortem?'

'I wish you didn't have to.' Webb's voice was savage. He dug his hands deep into his pockets. 'Damn. . . damn. . .'

'I wish no one had to,' Bonnie said gently. However angry this man had made her in the past, the anger was put aside now in the face of his pain. 'But your partner's family will want to know why this happened. . .'

'Oh, God. . .' Once again, Webb ran his hands through his hair. 'Ethel. . . I'll have to face her now.'

'Would you like me to talk to her?'

Webb shrugged. 'No. She's the wife of my friend. I have to see her.'

And Bonnie had to milk cows. She bit her lip, and cast one last long look up at Webb Halford.

'I'll leave you to it,' she said softly. 'I'd better go. And. . . And Webb?'

'Yes?'

'I'm sorry.'

He stared down at her for one long moment and then, as if an automatic reaction, his hand came out to touch her. It was a gesture of need—a plea for comfort—and Bonnie shouldn't have stepped back as if burned.

She did though. She closed her eyes in pain, turned and ran through the hospital gardens to her waiting car.

FREE BOOKS!
FREE GIFTS!
Play the "Lucky 7" Slot Machine Game!

**NO COST! NO OBLIGATION TO BUY!**
**NO PURCHASE NECESSARY!**

**PLAY "LUCKY 7"**
**AND GET AS MANY AS SIX FREE GIFTS...**

## HOW TO PLAY:

**1** With a coin, carefully scratch away the silver panel opposite. Then check the claim chart to see what we have for you - FREE BOOKS and gifts - ALL YOURS! ALL FREE!

**2** When you return this card we'll send you specially selected Love on Call novels and the gifts you qualify for, absolutely FREE. There's no catch. You're under no obligation to buy anything. We charge nothing for your first shipment. And you don't have to make any minimum number of purchases.

**3** After you've received your FREE books, if we don't hear from you, we will send you four brand new Love on Call novels to read and enjoy every month for just £1.99* each - the same price as the books in the shops. There is no extra charge for postage and packing and no hidden extras.

**4** The fact is thousands of readers enjoy receiving books through the post from the Reader Service. They like the convenience of home delivery... they like getting the best new novels at least a month before they're available in the shops... and they love their subscriber Newsletter, featuring author news, horoscopes, penfriends, competitions and much more.

**5** We hope that after receiving your free books you'll want to remain a subscriber. But the choice is yours - to continue or cancel, anytime at all! So why not take up our invitation - you'll be glad you did!

*Prices subject to change without notice.

NOT ACTUAL SIZE

*You'll look like a million dollars when you wear this lovely necklace! Its cobra-link chain is a generous 18" long, and the multi-faceted Austrian crystal sparkles like a diamond!*

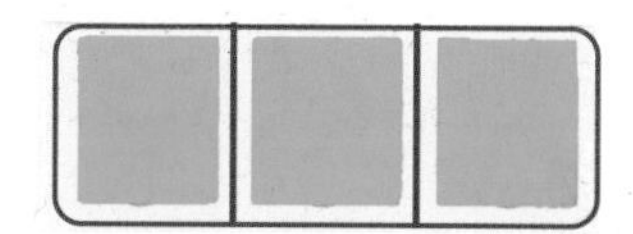

# Play "Lucky 7"

12A5D

Just scratch away the silver panel with a coin.
Then check below to see how many FREE GIFTS will be yours.

**YES!** I have scratched away the silver panel. Please send me all the gifts for which I qualify. I understand that I am under no obligation to purchase any books, as explained on the opposite page. I am over 18 years of age.

BLOCK CAPITALS PLEASE

MS/MRS/MISS/MR ______________________________

ADDRESS ______________________________

______________________________

POSTCODE ______________________________

**WORTH FOUR FREE BOOKS**
**PLUS A NECKLACE AND MYSTERY GIFT**

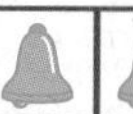

**WORTH FOUR FREE BOOKS**
**PLUS A MYSTERY GIFT**

**WORTH FOUR FREE BOOKS**

**WORTH TWO FREE BOOKS**

Offer expires 30th June 1996. We reserve the right to refuse an application.*Prices and terms subject to change without notice. Offer only valid in UK and Ireland and not available to current subscribers to this series. Overseas readers please write for details. Southern Africa write to: IBS, Private Bag X3010, Randburg 2125.

You may be mailed with offers from other reputable companies as a result of this application. If you would rather not receive such offers, please tick box. ☐

# CHAPTER SIX

HER two men were still sleeping soundly when Bonnie returned to the farm. The nurse came out to greet her, warned of her approach by the dogs, and reassured her.

'They haven't stirred, Dr Gaize. What's happening at the hospital?'

Her voice was raw with anxiety and Bonnie found herself wondering at the difference between city and country medicine. A drama in a community this small affected all players.

'And Dr Roberts dead. . .' The girl choked on tears as Bonnie finished speaking. 'He delivered me, you know. My mum always said he was one who put enjoyment before hard work, but he was always there when he was really needed. I can't believe he's dead.' She choked on a sob. 'And where's the town going to get another doctor. . .?' She took a deep breath, collecting herself, and when she spoke she was calmer. 'Well, I'll be off then, and let you get some sleep before your patients wake up.'

Fat chance, Bonnie thought bleakly. Seventy-three cows, bed bath and Paddy's shower, breakfast, washing. . .

Her weariness was almost a physical pain, battering her into the dust. As she milked the injured little Jersey by hand after completing the herd, she laid her head on the cow's warm flank and found her eyes closing all by themselves.

'Dr Gaize!'

Bonnie's eyes flew open and she gazed around with

a start of guilt. How long had she been dozing, for heaven's sake? The teats in her hand were dry and the cow was gazing down at her with lazy tolerance.

She rose unsteadily to her feet, fighting for her scattered wits. There were three people watching her from the yard gate—two men and a woman. What on earth must they think of her?

It seemed they knew exactly why she slept. Their eyes, as Bonnie approached, were warm with sympathy and understanding.

'Dr Gaize. . . Bonnie, I'm Neil Crammond.' The older man, burly and weather worn, held out his hand to grip hers. 'I doubt you'll remember us but we're your nearest neighbours.' He motioned to the woman beside him. 'This here's Grace, my wife, and this long layabout here is my son.'

The two gave Bonnie matching smiles. The family resemblance was striking and, although the woman was close to a foot shorter than her husband and son, the same good nature shone from her face.

'Eh, you're all done in, dear,' she said warmly. 'If we'd only known. . .'

'Well, we did, Mother,' Neil said strongly. 'We knew Henry Gaize was home from hospital. We just didn't know it was you who was looking after him, Bonnie lass. Doc Halford said his daughter had come and we assumed it was Jacinta.' He stood back from Bonnie and grinned. 'You've grown, girl, and no mistake, and you look the dead spit of your mother.'

Bonnie looked at them, dazed, trying to pull them back from a past she had tried to forget. Lois hadn't let Bonnie socialise in the neighbourhood. There hadn't been money for dresses or make-up, and when Bonnie wasn't studying she was needed at home to work. Still. . . She looked up at the young man and memory stirred.

'I went to school with you,' she said doubtfully.

'You did that,' the woman told her. 'It was a crying shame your aunt treated you like she did—and so I told Doc Halford this morning when he rang.'

'Dr Halford rang. . .'

'Of course he did.' It was Neil's turn to talk, cutting in on his wife's volubility. 'Told us just what was happening here. Of course, we'd thought it was Jacinta come back to spend time with her father—and there's not many round here that'd lift a finger to help Jacinta. But you, lass. . . Well, the community's been itching to give you a hand since you were ten.'

'And now we can,' the woman said in satisfaction. 'That's why we're here. Neil, unload the truck.'

'Unload. . .' Things were moving out of Bonnie's control. She spread her hands. 'Look, I don't know what Dr Halford told you. . .'

'He told us you've been running the farm and nursing two invalids and working yourself into the ground. And now. . .now he needs you in the hospital again because there's no one else and he's worried you'll drop dead on your feet. So——' she put her hands on ample hips and glared at Bonnie '—I'm a trained nurse though it's so long ago I can hardly remember my training but Doc Halford says the nursing required is bed baths, bossiness and common sense which I can still do——'

'Especially the bossiness,' her son broke in and grinned at his mother's glare.

'And Pete here is going to take over your milking for as long as your uncle's flat on his back—we're only milking thirty ourselves as we're changing to stud, so it's no bother. Neil's going to do whatever's needed round the place if Pete needs a hand and me. . .' The woman rolled her sleeves up with a martial light in her eye. 'I'm going to cook and clean and organise this place so that you can help Doc Halford and we won't have two doctors who both look like they're going to drop as dead as. . .as Doc Roberts.'

The thought of the old doctor made her give a fast, watery sniff and she turned quickly to hide a despised weakness. 'So there,' she said in a voice that wasn't quite steady. She fumbled on the floor of the truck cab for a casserole. 'Have you any arguments about that?'

Bonnie smiled. She did remember this woman—and she remembered fights with Aunt Lois that were not the least ladylike. She remembered a younger Grace Crammond handing her a parcel after school just after her mother had died, and Bonnie opening it to find a pretty, pretty party dress.

'It's because I knew and loved your mother,' Grace had said, but the memory had been lost in what ensued. Lois had confiscated the beautiful dress as being unsuitable and handed it to Jacinta. Jacinta had worn it to the school social and the next meeting between the women had been as loud as it was vituperative.

'I do know you, Mrs Crammond,' she said softly. 'I didn't. . . I'd forgotten you knew my mother.'

'Yeah, well. . .' Another watery sniff and then control was regained. 'She was my friend and she'd turn in her grave if she thought her daughter was being overworked with me not lifting a finger to help. As she's probably been turning in her grave for years at the way your aunt treated you. Now you can show me what has to be done and then you can put yourself to bed for two hours until eleven o'clock and then Doc Halford's expecting you at the hospital at eleven-thirty. Any objections?'

'I don't think I dare argue,' Bonnie said faintly and Neil and Pete Crammond both grinned.

'Very wise,' the older farmer told her. 'Off to bed with you, lass, and let Mother do her bossy best.'

Bonnie hadn't realised quite what a load was on her

shoulders until the Crammonds lifted it off.

It wasn't just the Crammonds either. By the time Grace Crammond woke Bonnie from an exhausted sleep at eleven there had been five lots of visitors, all bearing casseroles and offers of help.

'It's just as well Henry Gaize has a big freezer,' Grace told Bonnie, surveying the kitchen table in satisfaction. 'Because these two men are going to get nothing but my home cooking while I'm here, but if this lot keeps coming we should provide for Henry for months.'

'I don't. . .I don't understand.' Still thick with sleep, Bonnie regarded the table with awe.

'Word gets around,' Grace said darkly. 'Lois Gaize made the neighbours stay well clear of this place. With one action last night you've brought 'em back in droves.'

'The Bells are a popular family?' Bonnie asked and Grace nodded.

'They are that. And our poor Dr Halford. . . To lose his partner and then see the Bells in that condition—well, he and Trevor Bell are real good friends and it'll bring it all back. . .' She shook floury hands from her scone bowl and sniffed. 'Off you go now, dear. Doc Halford needs you, and they're saying you have to do the post mortem on poor old Doc Roberts. A dreadful thing to have to do, but if it'll set Ethel's mind at rest. . . She'd like to know there was some cause for this whole mess—something she can understand.'

'I hope I can tell her,' Bonnie said doubtfully. Sometimes post mortems were so inconclusive they were better left undone—especially if there was any trauma from the accident to disguise the underlying cause of death.

Bonnie pulled into the hospital car park fifteen

minutes later to find Webb Halford obviously waiting for her. The door of his surgery at the end of the building swung open and he strode across to meet her, his white coat flapping in the hot north wind.

'Thanks for coming,' he said brusquely and Bonnie managed to smile up into his exhausted eyes.

He looked as if he hadn't slept at all. His strong-boned face was haggard with exhaustion, and Bonnie wondered momentarily what Grace had meant when she had said 'it'll bring it all back'.

'I could hardly do anything but arrive promptly when you've organised me so thoroughly,' Bonnie told him, her eyes still on his face. 'I feel like I've been bulldozed.'

'Grace Crammond.' His tired eyes lit a little. 'She's a woman in a million. She was matron of this hospital for ten years before she met and married Neil—and I hear she runs her house on the same lines as she ran the hospital. Paddy and Henry will be organised to death.'

'She was force-feeding them fresh baked scones with jam and cream as I left,' Bonnie grinned. 'I've never seen two such willing victims.'

Webb returned her smile but the exhaustion and strain didn't lift, and Bonnie sensed where his thoughts lay.

'Show me where to go,' she said softly. 'I'll do this myself.'

'I'll help.'

Bonnie shook her head. 'No. Of all of you, I knew Dr Roberts the least. In fact I think I only met him once or twice in my life. This is something I can do. . .'

For you.

The words weren't said but they were implied. To do a post mortem on a friend was a harrowing experience and Bonnie could rid Webb of that duty. Despite the way he had acted, she still had cause to be grateful to Webb Halford.

Gratitude?

She looked up into his drawn, weary eyes and knew it wasn't gratitude she was feeling for this man. Marriage or no marriage, she'd fallen heavily, totally in love with Dr Webb Halford and there was nothing she wouldn't do to take the look of strain from his face.

Nothing?

It wasn't quite true. There was no way she was going to have an affair with Webb, she knew. He was married and he had a child—and marriage and family were sacred. No. . . She wouldn't let him make love to her—but if she could help him. . .

'Is there a medical history for Dr Roberts?' she asked, and Webb ran his hand wearily through his black hair and shook his head.

'Bill Roberts hasn't been examined for years. I looked up the files this morning. Ten years ago he had an examination by the previous doctor here who reported finding nothing wrong but slightly elevated blood pressure. Bill's been looking tired lately and I tried to get him to either let me examine him or see someone else, but he wouldn't have a bar of it. And now. . .'

'Show me where to go,' Bonnie said gently. 'The sooner it's done the sooner it's over.'

In the end it was a fast and relatively trauma-free procedure.

Dr Robert's body lay in the mortuary. In death the old man's face was serene, for all the world as if he had fallen asleep—which is what seemed to have happened, Bonnie thought as she read the notes provided by the police at the scene. A witness said Bill's car had veered into the centre of the road and then into the path of the oncoming car. The Bells had skidded sharply to one side, smashing into a tree, but Dr Roberts' car had come to rest some hundred yards further on without hitting a thing. The first people at the scene found him slumped over the wheel, quite dead.

He'd had high blood pressure. . .

It could mean anything when his blood pressure had last been taken ten years ago. After ten untreated years though. . . It could mean a stroke or a heart condition. . .

Bonnie stared thoughtfully down. There was nothing on the body to give her a clue. Nothing.

Finally she made a careful incision.

She needed to go no further. The sight of massive recent bleeding made her almost positive of what had happened and it took little further examination before she was able to close the incision with neat, surgical precision. Ethel Roberts would have her husband intact—he needed no further invasion of the sanctity of his death.

The aortic aneurysm must have been massive to have caused instantaneous death, Bonnie knew, sighing in relief at the news she could take to Ethel. The fact that Dr Roberts was travelling away from town when he died meant that he'd had no warning—if the aneurysm had bled slowly at first, he would have had crippling pain which would have made him at the very least stop the car and turn towards home.

Not such a dreadful death at seventy-five—to go out with no warning when he was still a busy, contented and respected member of a close community. . .

Bonnie gently lifted the sheet back over the dead face and filled in her notes for the coroner. Ethel could now bury her husband as soon as she wished.

Her task complete, Bonnie walked out of the mortuary and crossed to Webb's surgery. The findings might lift, fractionally, the look of strain on Webb's face—and it was Webb's place to tell Ethel.

Webb was seated behind his desk. His receptionist had obviously gone to lunch and as Bonnie entered she could see straight through to where he sat, his head in his hands and his shoulders slumped in a haggard gesture of defeat.

'Webb?' she said softly.

He looked up, his mouth twisting a little at the sight of her.

'Do you know you look about eleven?' he said and Bonnie grimaced.

'I feel about a hundred. Something about a night with no sleep. . .'

'If you're a hundred then I must be a hundred and fifty.' He paused, the faint smile fading from his eyes. 'You've been fast. What did you find?'

'An aortic aneurysm. Massive. It must have killed him almost instantly.'

He nodded and reached for the telephone. 'I'll tell Ethel.'

'Isn't it up to the coroner to release the findings?' Bonnie asked but Webb kept right on dialling.

'The coroner can sack me if he wants to,' he said grimly. 'Ethel's beside herself. She thinks her husband caused all that damage because he went to sleep at the wheel—and I can't convince her his death wasn't somehow caused by the accident. This, believe it or not, will make it a whole lot easier for her.'

'I can understand that.' That her husband's death had caused a tragedy was a lot easier to face than the fact that her husband himself had done damage.

'Do you want to go and see her? I'll look after things here. . .'

Webb shook his head. 'She's surrounded by relatives, and she's waiting for a telephone call.'

As Bonnie listened to him break the news to Ethel, she found herself wondering for the hundredth time what drove this man. He was capable of sarcasm and biting cruelty when he felt it was warranted—but the man speaking now was gentleness itself.

'I'll come and see you tonight after work,' he was telling the bereft woman on the end of the phone. Bonnie grimaced. After work. . . There wasn't going to be an 'after work' for Webb Halford for many weeks to come.

As if he read her thoughts Webb slowly placed the receiver down on the cradle and turned to her.

'I'm going to need help,' he said bluntly and Bonnie nodded.

'I know that.' She gave a rueful smile. 'I gather that's why you organised Grace Crammond.' She spread her hands. 'Of course I'm willing to help over the next few weeks.'

'It's not just the next few weeks I'm talking about.'

Silence. Bonnie sat back in her chair and looked down at her hands. 'I'm not. . .I'm not available for a long-term job,' she said at last.

'You won't consider being Kurrara's new GP?'

'I'm training to be a physician.' Bonnie's voice was a trifle breathless. 'I start in March. There's no way I'd consider a career change to come ho—— To come here.'

'To come home,' Webb corrected her. 'You were going to say it, Dr Gaize. Why didn't you?'

She met his eyes then with a gaze that was frank and direct. 'Because it's not my home. It never has been. I don't belong here.'

'Your mother was born here.'

'You know that?'

'Grace Crammond filled me in on your history this

morning when I rang her. She gave me an earful.' He grimaced. 'It's a shame I didn't ask Grace before I came charging in on you in Melbourne accusing you of neglect.'

'What did. . . What did Grace say?'

'That your mum left the district when she married. She says Henry's your mother's brother. Your mother and Henry were close, but your mum and Lois didn't get on. Then, when your parents died, your uncle insisted they adopt you and Lois did her duty by you in the worst possible way. Yet. . . Yet you do still think of this place as home, don't you, Bonnie?'

His gentle voice robbed her of her defences. Bonnie blinked back sudden tears and nodded. 'Y. . .yes. But I couldn't come back.'

'Because of the memories?'

'That's part of the reason.'

Webb nodded. 'I can understand that. I would just like. . . I'd like you to reconsider, that's all. I'm desperate for help now. Bill Roberts should have retired a couple of years ago, and he's been gradually winding down his practice. We started advertising for another partner eighteen months ago and so far have had two hopeless applicants—both of whom have been rejected by nearly every other town in the state. Doctors don't like country practice. They don't like the demands it puts on them, and its interference with their private lives.'

'So why are you here?' Bonnie asked curiously. 'You're not a Kurrara boy.'

'No.' Webb shook his head. 'I made a conscious decision to search for a job in a small community.'

'Why?'

Webb shrugged. 'Maybe you've heard that my wife was badly injured in a car crash some years ago. She couldn't cope with the strain of city life so we brought our little boy here. And now. . .well, Sam is happy as a pig in mud at the local school and Serena is content with her workshop and kiln—so it suits us all. But if I can't get anyone else. . .'

'Then Serena and Sam are not going to see very much of you,' Bonnie finished for him, and he shook his head.

'No.' He glanced at his watch. There was the sound of people arriving through Reception and Webb grimaced. 'Afternoon surgery already. Most people have rung up and cancelled unless it's urgent, but when you combine two doctors' practices then the urgent cases will fill one doctor's book.'

Bonnie nodded. 'So after organising me some free time—how can I help?'

'By agreeing to come here permanently.'

'Short of that.'

'You won't consider it?' He rose from his desk and came around to place a hand on her shoulder. The feel of his touch made Bonnie wince, but she held herself still with an effort. This man seemed to be seductive in his charm without even being aware of it—a man who used his attractiveness to get what he wanted with women. She found herself being sorry for the unknown Serena—to have a husband like this. . .

Sorry and green with envy at the same time.

'Please. . .' She bit her lip and stared down at her hands.

'What's wrong?'

'I don't. . .I don't like you touching me,' she whispered.

'Why the hell not?'

There was the hint of astonishment in his voice—as though touching her was something he enjoyed and he'd been sure the feeling was reciprocated. Bonnie stood and backed away from him.

'Because I don't like it,' she told him steadily. She glanced out at the rapidly filling waiting room. 'It seems. . .it seems your patients are coming early. Can I. . . Can I take some away from you?'

'Take surgery you mean?'

'Take surgery.'

Webb nodded, his eyes still puzzled. 'I'd like that.'

'If I do will you go home to bed?'

'And leave you working? That's hardly fair.'

'I'll go home at five tonight and leave you with the night shift,' Bonnie told him. 'There's no guarantee you won't be woken in the night and you know it.'

Webb hesitated, but the exhaustion behind his eyes was evident and the temptation was too great.

'If you really mean it. . .'

'I mean it.'

He lifted his hand to touch her but once more Bonnie backed away and Webb's eyebrows rose in a sardonic grin. 'I'm not planning to rape you, Dr Gaize.'

'You wouldn't get far if you were,' Bonnie told him icily. 'I have a black belt in judo.'

'You're kidding.'

'I'm not kidding.'

Webb shook his head in disbelief. 'You never got that at Kurrara.'

'I trained at university.'

'So. . . So if I walked over to you. . . If I were to place my hands on your shoulders and try and kiss you. . .?' There was an unmistakable gleam in Webb Halford's eyes and he took a step nearer.

'Don't try it.' Bonnie glanced desperately behind her. From the waiting room six pairs of eyes watched with avid interest.

'But you said you can defend yourself.' Webb's smile was pure mischief.

'If I have to, I will. Dr Halford, leave me alone!'

It was a cry of desperation and even before she uttered it she knew it was useless. There was no way Webb Halford was leaving her alone. He walked firmly two steps further, his hands came down on her shoulders and he leaned forward to kiss her.

Half a second later he was lying flat on his back.

The whole surgery burst into spontaneous applause. Bonnie looked out through the door and a slow flush crept over her face. Her audience, having heard the entire interchange, were riveted.

'I did warn you,' she told the recumbent figure on the floor.

'You did.' He grinned up at her, the relief from the tension of the past twenty-four hours finding release in blessed laughter. His grey eyes twinkled dangerously. 'You've hurt my back, Dr Gaize. You'll have to help me up.'

'Not likely.' Bonnie eyed his proffered hand with acute suspicion. Behind her, the occupants of the waiting room looked on agog.

'Don't you do it, dear,' an elderly woman chortled. 'He's having you on.'

'Don't I know it.'

'You assaulted me in front of witnesses in my own surgery.' Webb did his best to sound plaintive but it didn't quite come off. 'Help me up, Dr Gaize, or I'll sue you for every penny you possess. I'll even have the lawyers include one red sports car in my demanded payment. You'll be reduced to riding a secondhand bicycle.'

Still he didn't move from the floor and Bonnie nudged him with her toe.

'Get up. If you have no respect for your reputation. . .'

'My reputation. . . I've been floored by a woman. . .'

'Dr Halford, get up!'

'I'll lie here for the afternoon and let you consult around me if you don't help me up.' His laughter slipped. 'Honestly, Dr Gaize, I've damaged a disc or something. I think. . . You're going to have to help me up.'

Bonnie stared down. The laughter from the waiting room faded also as the patients watched their doctor with the first twinge of concern.

Bonnie too was becoming uneasy. He'd landed hard. . . If he had hurt himself. . . And surely he wouldn't pull her down with all these people watching. . .

She shrugged. Reaching down, she proffered a hand, and a second later she was on the floor on top of him.

'For heaven sake. . .' Bonnie didn't know whether to laugh or cry. This man was in his thirties—a respectable country general practitioner surrounded by his ailing patients and she was supposed to be here treating these patients. What on earth was this going to do to her image in the town? The entire waiting room was rocking with laughter, and Webb's receptionist, returning late from lunch, walked through the door and stood rooted to the spot in astonishment.

'Let me up,' Bonnie hissed frantically, fighting against his encircling arms. The laughter from the waiting room grew and Bonnie cringed. What on earth would Webb's wife say if she walked in now? What would the town make of this sort of behaviour from a married doctor?

'It'll cost you.'

He held her close, ignoring her struggles. Thank heaven she was wearing a divided skirt, Bonnie thought fleetingly—at least that part of her dignity had been spared.

'What will it cost me?' It was difficult to fight him

as she wished when she was conscious of all those eyes and the laughter. . .

'Dinner tomorrow night.'

'Dinner!' She drew back within his hold and glared. 'Dinner!'

'Serena and Sam are coming back tonight,' Webb told her. 'I've told them about you and they're dying to meet you. Serena suggested tomorrow and Grace says she'll Uncle and Paddy sit. . .'

'Serena. . . Grace. . . You mean you planned this?'

'I planned to ask you for dinner. I didn't intend to lie on the floor and ask you. Now we're here, however, I seem to have you at an advantage and a man would be a fool not to take it.'

'Take advantage you mean.'

'Take advantage,' he said solemnly. 'So. . . Dinner tomorrow, Dr Gaize?'

She pulled back against his hold.

'With Serena?' she asked suspiciously and Webb grinned.

'With Serena. And Sam. And our cat Christabelle and Sam's pet terrapin Mabel. My complete body-guard. Mabel's been known to glare from thirty paces at any upstart of a young doctor who dares to practise her judo on the likes of me. So. . . Do you agree, Dr Gaize?' Webb had moved into a sitting position, but he still held Bonnie firmly down. He looked around the waiting room. 'I don't see the lady has a choice, do you?'

The waiting room laughed and acquiesced. 'Go with him, love,' the old lady chortled. 'It'll do you both good and Serena's cooking's a treat.'

To meet Webb Halford's wife and child when she felt like this about him. . . Did he know what he was asking?

Maybe. . .maybe he did. Maybe this was a way she

could get their relationship back to where it should be—if she met his wife and child, and talked to him calmly and professionally over dinner. Maybe. . .

Who was she kidding?

'Dinner then, Dr Gaize?' Webb said silkily. He smiled at her and her heart gave the now familiar lurch. 'You'll stay on the floor until you agree.'

'I'll have dinner with you,' Bonnie snapped, hauling herself away and struggling to her feet. She looked around the waiting room and managed a smile. 'How you put up with this arrogant, overbearing, conceited male for a doctor until now. . .'

'He's all we've got,' an old lady told her, and the laughter slowly died from the waiting room as yesterday's tragedy drifted back. 'You'd better treat him kindly, love. He's all we've got.'

## CHAPTER SEVEN

BONNIE worked surgery straight through that afternoon and left as soon as she'd coped with the last inquisition from her final, curious patient. A new doctor—especially one with links to the town—was a glorious source of gossip and there wasn't one patient content to depart without hearing why Bonnie was back—and how long she intended staying.

How long?

As little time as possible, Bonnie thought grimly. This place was like a sticky web, drawing her in and keeping her tight. And at the centre of the web, weaving his Machiavellian plans, was Webb Halford.

She didn't sight the man again that day, for which her confused heart was grateful, but the following morning he telephoned as she finished eating Grace's breakfast.

'You don't have to be here,' Bonnie had protested to the Crammonds. 'Unless Webb needs me in Surgery I can cope.'

'And run yourself into the ground again? Not likely. And you needn't worry about us.' Grace Crammond had looked down at years of accumulated grime on the fire stove with a martial light in her eye. 'We're having fun.'

She was, and so were Henry and Paddy, Bonnie had to acknowledge. Grace pandered to them, bossed them and generally supervised their recovery with a measure of authority Bonnie couldn't even attempt, and Grace's menfolk gossiped to the two invalids as equals. Already Paddy looked fuller in the face, and Henry had been heard to laugh three times. It was into this scene of domestic harmony that Webb telephoned.

'Can you do this afternoon's surgery?' Webb asked brusquely when she answered on the third ring. 'I need to attend Bill's funeral.'

'Of course I will.' Most of the town would be at the doctor's funeral, and Grace had already warned Bonnie she'd be needed.

'Fine.' Webb sounded distracted and weary. 'I'll collect you at six from the rooms and bring you home for dinner.'

Dinner. . . She didn't want to go. She couldn't. . . 'Webb, I can't. Really. . .I can't ask Grace to look after Paddy and Henry. . .'

'Don't you worry about me,' Grace called from the kitchen, guessing the gist of the telephone call. 'Dr Halford's already fixed it with me.'

'You mean——' Bonnie stared at the telephone as if it were a nasty form of insect life '—you've already arranged. . .'

'See you at six,' Webb told her and the line went dead.

She was cut off.

Bonnie replaced the receiver, her heart numb. The best thing she could do was to cut Webb from her thoughts in the same way he'd cut the connection, but some things were impossible. She looked up at Grace Crammond, her eyes troubled. 'He's bulldozing you as well as me.'

The older woman shook her head. 'It's giving me a lot of pleasure to be bulldozed,' she assured Bonnie. 'Dr Halford told me he wants you to stay as his partner—and if I can add my mite to the persuasion. . .'

Bonnie gasped. 'You mean it's a plot to keep me here?'

Grace grinned. 'Doc Halford said he'd keep you

here if he had to seduce you to do it.' She chuckled at the look on Bonnie's face. 'He was joking, I guess, but you don't know what a pleasure it is to have the man joke. Our Dr Halford carries the weight of the world on his shoulders most times. With his little boy and Serena like she is. . .'

'What's. . .what's Serena like?' Bonnie asked cautiously. She shouldn't ask but the temptation was irresistible.

'Serena. . . Serena Halford's a very nice woman,' Grace said stoutly as though she didn't quite believe it. She looked across at Bonnie and gave a wry smile. 'Well, to tell you the truth, she's an artist with a world-wide reputation, and she fits in to this place like a bull in a shop full of her pottery. When she first came we all had doubts about her—but I'll say this—she's been a real good mum to little Sam—and even when she does flit off to foreign places she generally makes good arrangements for both Sam and the doctor. It's just. . . Well, Dr Halford looks so darn tired at times, playing mother and father to the little one. I could wish Serena was a bit more settled—but then I guess it's hardly fair.'

Bonnie nodded. A career woman for a wife. . . It fitted with Webb's penchant for taking comfort where he could—though she didn't have to like it.

Well, she'd meet Serena and then she could be icily cold to Webb's advances. If she was a friend to his wife. . . Surely, it would stop him touching her?

If only it could stop her wanting him, too.

She ran late with surgery. With unfamiliar patients and a filing system that was strange to her, every patient took longer than they ought. Bonnie was used to working with the hospital dispensary and limited brand names of medications—here she had to work with a copy of a Mims pharmaceutical manual at hand, and half her consulting time seemed to be flicking through its pages looking for the way a drug was dispensed. Even so, by the end of the afternoon she'd had three phone calls from the local pharmacist querying her prescriptions.

She saw her last patient out with relief, sighing with exhaustion. As she opened the door, Webb Halford unfolded his long frame from a waiting room chair and strode into her inner sanctum.

'All finished?'

'I hope so.' She slipped her white coat off and hung it behind the door and then wished she hadn't. Webb was looking down at her soft, cotton frock with admiration and all of a sudden she wished she was wearing jeans. And a turtle necked sweater. . . And army boots. . .

I'll be wishing for a suit of armour next, or at very least a chastity belt, she told herself with grim humour as she forced herself to meet his look.

'I just hope I haven't killed anyone.' She handed Webb a pile of consultation cards and tried to make her voice sound normal. 'No major problems, but a Mrs Harbent came in and wanted a repeat prescription for valium. She swore she gets it from you regularly but it's not on her card—so I told her she'd have to come back when you were here. She was furious.'

'She would be.'

'You don't prescribe it?'

'No. She demands it from every locum we ever get in the place, though. Usually I warn them, but I forgot to tell you. . .' Tiredness invaded his voice in a deadening wave.

'It doesn't matter.' Bonnie looked up into his face, longing to smooth away the worry lines on his forehead. He was still wearing his dark suit from the funeral, and it made him seem formal and somehow. . .somehow remote and defeated. This man carried the weight of the world on his shoulders, Grace had said, and maybe Grace was right.

'Ready for dinner?'

She nodded, her eyes still on his weary face. 'A bad funeral?'

'What do you think?' Webb held open the door while she collected her bag and then locked the door behind her. He dug his hands deep into the pockets of his trousers as he walked down the path. 'Is there ever a good one?'

'Some better than others,' Bonnie said diffidently. 'When it's someone's time to die then a funeral can almost be a celebration of the end of a long and happy life.'

'The problem is when it's not time.' There was real pain behind Webb's voice and Bonnie paused to look wonderingly up at him. 'And then every funeral afterwards brings it flooding back, over and over. And the look of pain on Ethel's face as we buried her husband. . .' He shrugged. 'Well, the longer the marriage I guess the greater the pain must be. So maybe. . . Maybe an early death's a blessing.'

'You can't love people without opening yourself to pain,' Bonnie whispered softly, almost to herself. 'That's why——'

'Why you cut yourself off from your family? Did it work?'

Bonnie shrugged. 'I guess. For a time. . . Only then there was Paddy. . . And now. . . And now I don't know how I can walk away from Henry again.' And I don't know how I can walk away from you, her mind whispered, but some thoughts were best kept to herself.

'You don't have to walk away from Henry,' Webb told her.

'No?'

'Move in with Henry and practise medicine here.'

'I doubt Henry would approve of that.' Bonnie grimaced. 'When he's well he won't want me any more. You'll see.'

'Are you so sure?'

'I'm not exactly a wanted person.' It was hard to keep the bitterness out of her voice and Bonnie gave a slight gasp as she heard herself utter the words. Heaven knew she wasn't looking for sympathy.

'Bonnie. . .' Webb stopped dead, turning to grasp her shoulders, and they stood motionless in the fading light. 'I don't think you should say that.'

She shrugged. 'It's true.'

'And if I said I wanted you?'

'Then I'd say that it's pure cupboard love. You want a new doctor for Kurrara.'

'Not only that.'

'Well, that's the only sort of desire I understand,' Bonnic said flatly. What other sort of desire could there be when the man was married? 'And I'm not—repeat, not—going to set up practice here. Now. . . Now are your family waiting for dinner?'

Webb kept hold of his grip on her shoulders. If anything, his grip tightened and Bonnie refused to try and pull away. Hold yourself still, her heart told her. Hold yourself still because to do anything else in this charged atmosphere is to invite disaster.

'You were engaged last time you came home?' Webb said at last.

'You've been doing your homework.' Still there was bitterness in Bonnie's voice. She couldn't keep it at bay.

'What happened?'

'He ended it.'

His dark eyes softened. 'I see.'

He didn't. How could he see the hurt, added to all the other losses in Bonnie's young life, that Craig's betrayal had caused?

'Bonnie, there's a time to start anew,' Webb said gently, the hold on her arm easing. 'Of all people, I should know. . .'

'I don't think I'm interested in your past love life,' Bonnie said sharply. 'Look, is Serena waiting with dinner, or isn't she?'

He sighed. 'Ever practical. And you're right of course, oh sensible Dr Gaize. Serena is waiting and so is dinner, and a spoiled dinner and an angry Serena is a combination to be reckoned with. Can we drive your car?'

Bonnie stared. 'But I thought you lived just behind the hospital?'

'I do,' Webb grinned. 'Two hundred yards away. But I don't give invitations to a woman with a car like this in order to walk! Three turns around the block before dinner, Bonnie Gaize, or dinner's off.' His smile deepened as a small, black-haired imp flew around the corner of the hospital and headed for Webb at a run. 'And if I'm not mistaken, we have a passenger. Sam, this is Dr Gaize. Dr Gaize—my son.'

'The lady who owns the Noddy car.' The little boy had eyes only for Bonnie's bright red sports car. He was about five years old, with his father's shock of pitch-black hair, huge appealing eyes, and shorts and T-shirt that looked like they'd seen much better days. 'Please, please, can I have a ride in it?'

'The Noddy car!' Bonnie chuckled. 'The salesman would have kittens at your description, but if that's what you want. . .'

It definitely was. Sam Halford, it seemed, had been

lying in wait for this very opportunity. He bounced his small body into the car before Bonnie finished her sentence.

Ten minutes later, with Sam's appetite for open-air motoring sufficiently sated, the little car came to a stop outside Webb's home.

'It's a great car,' Sam said shyly. He met Bonnie's direct look with eyes that were searching. What he saw in her answering look seemed to reassure him. 'Will you let us have more rides in it? Dad and me?'

'We'd like that,' Webb added, his hand on his son's tousled head. 'We've been looking for a lady with a Noddy car for quite some time, haven't we, Sam?'

And what the heck was that supposed to mean? Webb's accompanying smile was bland as cream—no reason at all for Bonnie's heart to lurch so sickeningly. She took a deep breath, fought for control and turned to greet Webb's wife.

Serena was waiting on her front step.

Webb's wife was blonde and dishevelled, clad in floral overalls stained with clay and paint. The lady waved a soup ladle as they walked towards her. She smiled a smile which matched Webb's for charm and came forward to take both Bonnie's hands in hers.

'Hi, Bonnie.' She drew back a hand to wipe her cheek with her fingers, as if she'd suddenly felt a blob of paint there. The action smeared a dab of yellow down one cheek—to charming effect. 'I'm really, really happy to meet you.' She flicked a mischievous glance at Webb. 'Though we've heard so much about you we feel we know you already, don't we, Sam?'

'My dad said you have a cute nose and freckles and we'll really, really like you, and he says you can't shoot a cow, and you've lost a chook and you can't find it anywhere, but you give an anaesthetic like a. . .like a Trojan. . .' Sam announced. 'What's a Trojan, Dad?'

'Not someone heavily into giving anaesthetics,' Webb grinned.

'And you helped make my friend Sophie better,' Sam announced as though it clinched his good opinion entirely and Bonnie's eyes flew to Webb's.

'The Bells. . . You've heard of their progress from Melbourne?'

'I've heard from Melbourne.' Webb's smile warmed her through and through. It was intimate and intense—not the smile a happily married man should give a guest at all. 'The Bells will be fine—all of them, though Trevor's in for a long period of rehabilitation. Their internal injuries were minimal. Sophie will need some plastic surgery but it looks like it may be minor. So. . . One piece of good news.' He turned, still smiling, to his urchin son. 'Now are you intending to wash before dinner or come to the table in all your multicoloured dirt like someone else I could mention?' He looked meaningfully across at the placidly smiling Serena.

Serena chuckled, looking ruefully down at herself. 'Oh, help. I always forget to change. Do you mind me in my dirt, Bonnie?'

'I think I like it.'

Bonnie thought she liked the whole place.

As she was ushered inside, Bonnie could see at a glance why the ladies of Kurrara eyed Serena askance. This was no normal household. It was crammed to bursting point with artistic efforts in various stages of production, and one could hardly move without shifting a statue or urn. It was a friendly, colourful jumble, however, and someone here was taking Christmas very seriously indeed. Invading a good third of the living room was the biggest Christmas tree Bonnie had ever seen in a private house, magnificently and artistically draped all in white and silver. The only exception to white and silver was yards and yards of threaded, multicoloured popcorn standing out vividly against the green and white, and high in the branches, one glittering angel with star held aloft.

'I did the popcorn ropes,' Sam said anxiously, tucking his hand into Bonnie's. 'Do you like them?'

'I love them. And the smell. . .'

'Pine needles,' Serena said in satisfaction. 'Added to roast chook. Unless your lost chook has put you off poultry?'

'This one's name's not Frankie, is it?' Bonnie asked and they all laughed.

'It's named Ingles Chicken Size 15,' Serena grinned. 'I swear. Chook rustling's not my scene.'

Chook cooking certainly was, however, and to Bonnie's amazement she ended up having a lovely, happy meal, Serena and Sam leaving her in a constant ripple of amusement.

Webb said little. He sat at the head of the table and watched the two women and his son with the air of a benevolent genie. He was tired to the point of exhaustion, Bonnie could see, but somewhere during the relaxed meal the look of strain slipped away to be replaced by something more enigmatic.

His eyes seldom strayed from Bonnie, and Bonnie was aware of them—burningly aware. A couple of times she turned to him to find the look in his eye almost possessive.

How could he look like that at her when Serena was just there—so close? It made her feel uncomfortable and frightened—how could she feel like this and feel such strong affection towards Serena at the same time? The ultimate betrayal. . .

It was almost a relief when the telephone interrupted their coffee and Webb rose to answer it. He came back to the table, the mask of tiredness slipping once more into place.

'Ron Coltman's bringing his little boy in with cuts to his head. I'll go across and see what the damage is. Finish your coffee, Bonnie.'

Bonnie was already standing. 'I'll go,' she told him. 'You're exhausted.'

'I'm fine.' His brow snapped into a curt rejection. 'Finish your coffee.' He was gone before she could argue further.

Serena sighed and rose, methodically clearing plates, and Bonnie automatically moved to help her. Sam had been sent off to bathe and could be heard noisily splashing and singing from the bath tub.

'Thank you for coming tonight,' Serena said gently as she ran the dish water. 'It's done Webb good.'

'To have company?'

'To have you here,' Serena told her. She shrugged her hands in the soapy water. 'He gets little enough pleasure. . .'

'He took the funeral hard,' Bonnie said cautiously, and Serena nodded.

'Yes. I don't think that's anything he'll ever get over.' She turned impulsively to Bonnie and held out soapy hands. 'You won't reject staying here without really careful thought, will you, Bonnie? Webb wants you to stay so much! We all do.'

This lady didn't know what she was saying. Bonnie stared at her, her eyes reflecting confusion and misery and Serena swore under her breath.

'Oh, Bonnie. Don't look like that. It's not fair to put pressure on you, I know. It's just. . . It's just I do love Webb so much and it breaks my heart to see him under the strain he's under. And now. . . With only one doctor. . .'

So stay home from your international travels, Bonnie thought savagely, but wouldn't have uttered the thought for the world. It wasn't fair either—that

Serena sacrifice her career for Webb's. It was just. . . If it was Bonnie married to Webb, how could she bear to leave him?

The phone rang again, breaking into her thoughts, and Serena crossed to answer it. Once again Serena swore.

'Thus endeth a perfectly good night,' she grimaced. 'The cut needs stitching under anaesthetic, which means Webb needs you, Bonnie.' She sighed dramatically. 'And that leaves me with the dishes. You doctors. . . The life-and-death imperative—it dumps me with the dishes every time.'

'Leave them for later,' Bonnie smiled. 'We'll come back.'

'Not likely,' Serena said darkly. 'If there's dishes in the sink Webb will produce every medical emergency under the sun—and I'd rather do the dishes than have the district with more drama in its midst. Off with you to save lives!' She shoved her arms up to her elbows in soap suds and groaned theatrically. 'I know my place.'

'I don't actually see your place in the kitchen sink,' Bonnie said cautiously and Serena flicked a soap bubble at her.

'You're dead right.' Her face grew serious for a moment. 'Do consider carefully, Bonnie,' she told her. 'You don't know. . . You don't know just how much Webb needs someone like you.'

The cut was a nasty one, a jagged slice from broken glass into the top of a three-year old's scalp.

'He was watching me through the window,' his father told Bonnie as she hurried into Casualty. Webb was bent intently over the small child, and the father seemed desperate to explain the accident to anyone who would listen. 'I'm trying to build a cubby house before Christmas. We've told the kid it's a tool shed but Grant's a smart little button and he has his suspicions. Anyway, the wife was in the kitchen and Grant was supposed to be watching television—but he sneaked up to the front room to look out at what I was doing. There's an armchair in front of the window—and the next thing the whole chair tips and Grant comes straight out through the glass.'

'It could have been a lot worse,' Webb said gently, his fingers still carefully probing. The child was semi-conscious, whimpering with pain in the arms of his blood-spattered, white-faced mother. 'It seems he's tipped almost upside down before he went through—so he hit the back of his scalp first and protected his eyes.'

'Dear heaven,' the man said weakly. 'If he hadn't. . .'

It didn't bear thinking of. The woman choked on a sob and her arms tightened around her precious bundle.

'Why isn't he awake then, Doc?' the father demanded.

'He's lost a lot of blood.' The nurse came through with the requirements for the drip and Webb signalled for Bonnie to take over. 'Can you take Mr and Mrs Coltman through to the waiting room and make them a good strong cup of tea?' Webb asked the nurse. He lifted the unprotesting child from his mother's arms and laid him gently on the trolley. The child's lack of protest showed Bonnie just how much blood he had lost. 'We're going to put Grant to sleep now and stitch his head—and I doubt if either of you really want to watch.'

'He'll be. . .' The mother couldn't go on. Her knees buckled and she leaned heavily on her husband's arm.

'He'll be fine,' Webb assured her. He smiled reassuringly at the deathly pale woman and his hand touched her shoulder in a gesture Bonnie was starting to know. 'I promise. Dr Gaize and I will take good care of him.'

Once they were alone what had to be done was a simple enough procedure. A similar cut on an adult might be stitched under local anaesthetic, but not on such a little one, where he might struggle at any moment.

'Maybe if his mum stayed we could try,' Bonnie ventured but Webb shook his head.

'She darn near passed out before you arrived,' Webb told her. 'If I'm half-way through stitching and she loses consciousness it'll frighten Grant a lot more than he's frightened now.' He took the little boy's hand into his. The child, beyond understanding, gazed up at him with pain-filled, bewildered eyes.

'You know you copped a fair whack on your head, young man. I guess that's what happens to young men who try to outsmart Father Christmas. We're patching you up right now—and that's why you're getting so sleepy. . .'

The sedation and loss of blood made Webb's words almost unnecessary. Grant was past worrying. Bonnie slipped an anaesthetic in as Webb scrubbed, but he hardly needed it.

The procedure was swift and sure. Under anaesthetic, Webb cleaned the wound with care, ensuring the cut was scrupulously clean and free from splinters of glass. The cut was a deep, jagged slice and Bonnie hated to think what could have happened if he hadn't somehow turned to protect his eyes.

Thirty tiny stitches later, Webb nodded to Bonnie and she reversed the light anaesthetic. The child stirred in moments and Sister brought the anxious parents back in.

'We'll keep him in hospital overnight,' Webb told them. He smiled compassionately at the drawn faces of the child's parents. 'Sister can make beds for you, if you'd like to stay. It's a good twenty-minute drive back to your farm, and I doubt if either of you are up to driving.'

'We'd like that. . .' The woman's face crumpled and she took Webb's hand. 'Thank you. . .'

'You have to thank Dr Gaize,' Webb told her. 'Without Dr Gaize we would have had to ambulance Grant thirty miles to the nearest anaesthetist and surgeon.' He grimaced. 'We'll have to do that for future casualties if she decides not to stay.'

More pressure. Bonnie's anger rose as she calmly bade the parents good night.

'That's not fair,' Bonnie said savagely as they finally walked away from the Coltmans' hearing. 'It's not right that you should pressure me like this.'

'You have blood on your dress,' Webb told her, holding the door open for her to pass through. Behind them the little one was passing into a heavy, natural sleep with Sister on guard, as well as his parents.

'It doesn't matter.' Bonnie stood on the hospital steps and took a long, calming breath of the warm night air. 'It'll come out. . .'

'It'd be a shame if it didn't.' Webb turned her to face him. They stood in the doorway, the illumination from the building lighting their faces with a tinge of fluorescent hue. Inside the entrance to Casualty was yet another Christmas tree and its flickering glow made the light seem strange and unreal. Like the streets of a big city, Bonnie thought fleetingly—neon lights and people and bustle—not the steps of a small country hospital in the heart of rural Australia.

The streets of London. . . She should be in London. Not here! Not with this man.

'I have to go,' she said tightly, her breath coming fast. She felt she was almost choking. He was so darned close—his gentle, skilled hands holding her with the tenderness he'd used on the child's mother and the sensation was threatening to overwhelm her. 'Paddy. . . Henry. . .'

'Grace is coping admirably with Paddy and Henry, and loving it,' Webb told her, his voice softening even further. 'And we have things to sort out, Bonnie Gaize. You and I. . .'

'Things?' She ventured a look up at him and it was a major mistake. He was watching her with the same expression he had watched her with over dinner—a mixture of compassion, wonder and emotion. A strange, haunting look that pierced Bonnie to the bone—that made her want to weep for something she could never have—that she could never even dream of having. 'I don't. . .I don't know what you mean. . .'

'I think you do.' His hold tightened.

'Webb, let me go,' Bonnie said breathlessly. 'Please. . . If someone comes through the door now. . . Please. . .'

'If someone comes through the door now they'll see that I'm kissing the most desirable woman within a thousand miles of this place,' Webb told her firmly. 'Because that's just what I intend doing.'

'No. . .'

'Yes.' And before she could utter a protest his arms pulled her closer and she was ruthlessly, thoroughly kissed.

No!

The word screamed itself over and over into Bonnie's confused heart. She held herself rigid in his arms, steeling herself not to respond to those seductive lips, while images of Serena and Sam kaleidoscoped round and around her confused mind. No. . .

She put her hands up and pushed with all her might, but his hold tightened.

'Give in to this, Bonnie,' he growled huskily into her hair and pulled her slight frame in tighter against him. 'You want this as much as I do. I can feel it.'

'No!'

It was a real scream this time, a scream of distress and denial. She wouldn't do this. He couldn't make her. No matter how much her crazy, errant heart was wanting this man, she had no right. . . No right. . .

And neither had he. How dared he do this to her? Was this some crazy ploy to make her stay here—as his mistress, for heaven's sake?

'Bonnie. . .' There was a hint of uncertainty in his voice and he took a step back, holding her at arm's length. 'Bonnie, love. . .'

'I am not your love.'

His hands began to tighten again, refuting her statement with action, but Bonnie would have none of it. She writhed out of his grasp and stood just out of his range, breathing like a woman who'd just run a marathon.

'Leave me alone,' she gasped. 'Webb, no. . .'

'You don't want me to.'

'Yes, I do!' She held up her hands to ward him off. 'How can you imagine I would want this?'

His dark eyebrows snapped down in a frown. 'I'm not wrong though, am I, Bonnie? This thing I feel. . . You feel it too, and if it's mutual then what could possibly be wrong. . .?'

What could possibly be wrong?

'You cruel, conceited, two-timing, double-crossing. . .' Fury rose in a crimson flame, engulfing Bonnie and robbing her of further speech. What could possibly be wrong? 'Of all the immoral. . .'

His face was still before her, the dark eyes blank with incomprehension. Incomprehension? Could he really not understand? He lifted a hand as if to touch her and all of a sudden it was too much. Bonnie's hand lifted as well, she pulled back and delivered the hardest slap she had ever dealt in her life. It hurt her hand to deliver it, and the sound reverberated around and around the stillness of the hospital car park.

'You unscrupulous toad,' she spat at him. She fished frantically in her pocket for her car keys and magically they were there. She held them before her like a talisman, warding off evil. 'I'm going home now, Webb Halford, and don't you dare stop me. I'm not coming near here again, either. You can tell Mrs Crammond—or I'll tell her myself—that she's no longer needed to care for Paddy and Henry. I don't care about this town or its medical emergencies—at least not enough to compromise what I believe to be right. I'm not working in your hospital. I'm staying home looking after Paddy and Henry and if you come near the farm I'll. . .I'll set the dogs on you. Now leave me alone or I'll scream the hospital down—and then where will your precious reputation be, Dr Webb Halford? Not that you seem to care one jot about it anyway. You don't deserve to have a wife and a son ever. . .ever. . .'

Bonnie's voice broke on a sob and she turned and ran.

## CHAPTER EIGHT

GRACE was placidly knitting when Bonnie arrived back at the farm, a dog sleeping soundly over each slippered foot. She looked up at Bonnie's tear-stained face, drew her own conclusions and carefully didn't comment.

Neither did she comment when told Bonnie would no longer be working for Webb.

'Thank you for your help,' Bonnie told the middle-aged nurse in a voice that refused to stay steady. 'I really appreciate it. But I'll do my own milking tomorrow, so I don't need you to come.'

'Well, I'll let Pete sleep in tomorrow, then,' Grace told her, calmly gathering her belongings into her capacious handbag. 'But I've stripped down one side of the Aga and I'm blessed if I'll stop with the job half-done. So I'll be back in the morning, like it or lump it, miss.'

'But tomorrow's Christmas Eve. You'll have your own work. . .'

'I'm doing this for Henry,' Grace told her, her kindly eyes resting thoughtfully on Bonnie's face. 'I never knew your uncle until now—and it seems that maybe we've judged him hard.' She sniffed. 'And maybe we didn't judge your aunt hard enough.' She gave Bonnie a swift hug and smiled warmly at her. 'Now you get some sleep, lass, and try not to dwell on what's worrying you. Maybe a few cows tomorrow morning is what you need. A nice placid time in the dairy after a good sleep. . .'

Sleep. . .

Impossible, Bonnie thought as she twisted in her

bed, but her tired mind finally took its own course and she drifted into troubled slumber. She woke at one and three to turn Henry, then at five she turned him again before she started milking. Her uncle stirred, accustomed by now to his regular turnings, and took her hand in a strong grip.

'It's good to have you here,' Bonnie,' he whispered into the half-light. 'Good. . .'

That should be some comfort, Bonnie thought, but it didn't give the comfort it should. It was the first time Henry had ever expressed his feelings towards her, and she found herself doubting his meaning almost as much as she doubted Webb.

All of them. . . When had they ever meant what they said? Her parents had told her they loved her and then deserted her. Craig. . . Well, the less she thought about Craig the better. Then Henry, and now Webb. . .

It wasn't safe to give her heart. It caused only exposure and ultimate pain. When would she ever learn to keep herself armour-plated against love?

The cows plodded placidly into their bails as the morning milking progressed, and Bonnie learned Grace's dictum was true enough. There was a measure of peace to be gained in the dairy, with the dawn light breaking over the distant hills, the cows' gentle lowing and the magpies warbling in the gums above her head.

She could stay here. . . If it wasn't for Webb Halford she could stay. . .

She gave her final cow a pat on its rump as it ambled from the bails and looked up to find Webb Halford, tranquilly watching her from the top rail of the yard.

How long had he been there?

Heaven alone knew. Bonnie had hardly looked out into the yard. The cows, at this stage of the year, were settled enough to bring themselves into the bails as required, as eager to be rid of their milk as Bonnie was to relieve them of it. She'd hardly stirred from the dairy as she milked. Now, as she walked out into the yard, hose in hand ready to clean down the concrete yard, she looked up and there he was.

'What. . .what do you want?'

'I know you said you'd set the dogs on me if I came near the place.' Webb smiled a tranquil smile, removed a piece of straw from his mouth and flicked it aside. 'Both dogs met me when I drove in. I told them what was expected of them, but Mrs Crammond offered them breakfast and they lost interest in savaging doctors—or deceiving husbands for that matter.'

Bonnie stood rooted to the spot, all colour draining from her face. Webb sat motionless on the rail, his shirt open at the collar, the soft wind ruffling his dark hair—and his eyes smiling at her as though she were being embraced.

Deceiving husbands. . . How could he sit there and say it, for all the world to hear?

'Get out of here,' she whispered. 'Get out. . .'

'No.'

'Webb. . .'

He swung himself down from the rail, then, in one lithe movement and strode across the yard. Bonnie was wearing her uncle's gum boots and she backed awkwardly, but swiftly for all that. She lifted her hand and found she was still holding the hose.

'Get away. . .'

'Or you'll shoot me?' He grinned. 'That's a hose you're holding, not a gun.'

It would have to do. The hose was a high-powered jet, fitted with a trigger nozzle. Bonnie held it high, clenched her fingers tight around the trigger, closed her eyes and squeezed. A blast of water streamed out and hit Webb straight in the chest.

Webb's stride didn't falter. Neither did his smile. He came on regardless, the water blasting fiercely against him with increasing intensity as he neared her.

'Get away!' Bonnie backed again. As she did, her foot slipped in a fresh cow pat. The next minute Dr Bonnie Gaize was flat on her back in cow dung, a stream of water spraying uselessly upward and down again over her face.

'Well, well. . .' Webb reached her then and stood, laughing down at his helpless lady. His eyes were full of wicked enjoyment. 'I seem to have the upper hand, my Bonnie. Or the upper something.'

Bonnie's fingers eased on the trigger and the spray died. She lay helpless in the dung and mud, torn between a desire to cry and an absurd, hysterical wish to laugh.

She must be hysterical. She must. . . Dear heaven, the way this man looked at her.

'Dr Gaize, you've fallen in cow dung,' Webb told her politely. 'It appears, from this angle, to be squelching out the sides. I'm not sure if I wish to investigate further.'

'You toad. . .'

'You told me I was a toad last night,' he agreed. 'It didn't make sense at the time. Stand up.'

'You. . .'

'Are you intending lying in cow dung for the rest of the day? It's not my ideal choice of bed—but then I guess city doctors have different ideas from us country folk.' He removed the hose from her nerveless fingers, put down a hand to grasp hers and hauled her to her feet. Then he twisted her so she was turned away from him. 'Stand still.'

'You. . .'

A blast of cold water hit her hard in the small of her back. Bonnie yelped in shock, but Webb held the hose ruthlessly close, spraying away the dung from her jeans and shirt.

She stood stock still, shock rendering her powerless. The water streamed over her as she tried to make her mind think, but it was no good. She didn't have the strength to run—and how could she run from this man? How could she?

Finally the flow of water ceased.

'That's better,' Webb approved. He let the hose fall from his hand and then twisted Bonnie around so she was facing him. 'I don't like my women coated in cow dung, however much they approve the coating.'

'You toad.'

'You keep saying that,' he told her. 'I would have thought a good judo throw would be in order now, instead of a bleating protest, wouldn't you?'

Bonnie bit her lip. A judo throw against a much larger opponent could work when he wasn't expecting it, but now. . . What would ensue would be a wrestling match, and she had a sneaking suspicion that Webb Halford would relish it. She also had a sneaking suspicion who would win.

'Very wise,' he told her softly, his eyes twinkling in understanding.

'Webb, please. . .'

'Please don't touch me? Why not, Bonnie?'

She stood, sodden and dripping, her waist gripped by his strong, capable hands and she was powerless to do any more than shake her head helplessly, tears starting behind her eyes.

'Bonnie, after you flung yourself off in a temper last night I thought over what had happened.' The laughter had suddenly faded and Webb's voice softened. His eyes held hers, and they were deadly serious. 'It didn't make sense. Then the words started separating—the stream of abuse you hurled at me. Two-timing. . .

Double-crossing. . . Immoral. . . A toad I might well turn out to be, Bonnie Gaize, but the other three adjectives you'll have to justify. Now, Bonnie—before you leave this yard.'

'You are. . .' she whispered.

'I'm not.' His voice was flat and final. 'I'm not two-timing or double-crossing anyone—unless you call kissing you a betrayal of a wife who's been dead for three years.'

'Dead?' Bonnie gazed blankly up at him, her wet face white with incomprehension and pain. 'Dead? But. . . But Serena's not dead.'

Any faint, lingering doubts washed away from Webb's face. His grip tightened. 'I thought as much.' He pulled her soaking body into his and there was the beginnings of triumph in his voice. 'I should have squirted you harder, my adorable Bonnie. How dare you think I'd make love to a woman when I have a wife and child—much less take my new love home to meet them?'

'But. . . But Henry told me. . .'

Webb pushed her away from her and held her at arm's length. The laughter died once again from his face, and his deep grey eyes met hers with absolute conviction.

'I don't know what your uncle told you,' he said softly. 'At a guess your uncle has been isolated and incommunicative for the entire time I've been in this town—and he only knows what he's seen, not what he's heard.'

'And. . . And he's wrong?' Was it crazy to let the tiny flicker of hope flare and grow?

'Bonnie, my wife's name was Diana, not Serena.' Webb's hands were still caressing her. 'We met and married when we were at university and we loved each other very much. Then. . . Then four years ago, when

Sam was tiny, Diana crashed her car, irreparably damaging her liver. Diana always dreamed of bringing Sam to live in the country, so. . .so for the last year of her life we came here. We came where she could lie in the garden and watch the sun set over the valley, and know that Sam was safe and in a secure environment for the rest of his life.'

'But. . .' This wasn't making sense. Bonnie's head was whirling and Webb's grip tightened, sensing her need. 'But Serena?'

'Serena is my sister, my twin in fact, although she hardly looks like me. When Diana was dying, Serena packed up her city studio and announced she'd work here. I didn't have the financial resources to stop work to look after Diana and Sam, but between us. . .well, without Serena I think I would have gone mad. Even with. . .' His voice faded and Bonnie looked wonderingly up into the pain-filled eyes. 'Well, it's been a nightmare from which I never thought I could emerge—until one day I walked into a city hospital and met a woman with a snub nose and freckles and a heart as big. . .'

'No!'

'Yes,' he said softly and kissed her lightly on the forehead. 'You're nothing like Diana. Nothing, and I thought I could never fall in love again because there would never be another Diana. Only there doesn't have to be. Because there's a Bonnie, and she has a black belt in judo, for heaven's sake, and she falls over in cow dung and tries hard not to laugh when she should be angry and she breaks her heart over missing chooks and injured cows and she's been treated despicably and somehow. . .somehow I'm going to make her see that she is loved for her wonderful self, and that we can be a family. You and me, Bonnie Gaize, and all our various appendages. What do you say?'

He was looking straight into her eyes. The water from his damp, dark hair was trickling down over his face and the moisture droplets glistened in the morning sun. Bonnie's heart twisted inside her, melting at this man's pain—at his need, and the love she saw in his eyes.

'Oh, Webb. . .I can't. . .'

'You can't say you'll marry me right now?' he said seriously. 'I can understand that. A girl may need an acquaintance of a little more than a week before such a momentous decision. I'm a patient man. I can afford to wait.'

'No!'

'You mean I don't have to wait?'

'Webb. . .'

He shook his head, his eyes once more twinkling at her. 'OK, Bonnie, forget the proposal of marriage for just this moment. We'll put it off for twenty minutes at least. You're not going to demand that I don't kiss you though?'

'Webb, no!'

'Just as well,' he said darkly, and bent to do just that.

'No!'

He lifted his head again, his eyes astonished. 'What is it, my love?'

'We can't. Please. . .'

Webb gazed around. From the other side of the gate, the little Jersey cow whose leg had been dislocated surveyed the entwined pair with benign interest.

'Oh, I see.' Webb chuckled, his face almost boyish. 'Our patient is up to poking her nose into other people's business again. Recovering nicely, I see.'

'Webb. . .'

'You're very right, my love.' Webb shook his head in mock disapproval at the cow and turned back to Bonnie. 'I didn't realise we were on such public display, and the shock of what I'm about to do might bring on a relapse in the most recovered of patients. But never fear—I know just the place. I'll show you I'm a real country boy at heart.' And with one swift movement he swung Bonnie high in his arms, oversized gum boots and all, and was striding out through the yard and across the cattle grid to the shed beyond before she could utter a squeak of protest.

At this time of year the haystack was almost full, with a few bales hauled from one corner to feed injured stock. The corner formed the basis of rough steps up to the heights, and Webb didn't stop. Bonnie writhed in his grasp but she was firmly ignored.

'Put me down!'

'It's a long drop to the bottom,' he warned. 'If I were you I'd stay still.'

His long legs carried his prize higher, higher until they reached the top, under the sun-warmed iron roof, and where the loosened wisps of hay made a bed fit for kings.

'A country boy,' Webb said in soft satisfaction as he set down his precious burden. 'About to kiss his country girl.'

Bonnie had gone beyond protest. She was dripping wet, one gum boot had been lost somewhere between the dairy and haystack, and the other had tumbled downward during Webb's climb. She lay barefoot and bewildered where Webb placed her on the hay, and she could only watch, her eyes enormous, as Webb followed her tenderly down.

'If you knew how beautiful you look,' he whispered tenderly as his mouth lowered onto hers. 'If you only knew how much I've waited for this. . .'

And then there was no room for any words between them. There was his mouth on hers, his hands caressing her lithe figure, the damp fabric of her shirt proving no barrier to sensation. He lay full length beside her, and took her into his arms in a sweeping, all-possessing gesture that brooked no protest.

And Bonnie would make none. She couldn't.

This felt so right. This felt as if she had finally come home—as if this man was part of her, and here was her place.

Her lips opened, welcoming the pressures of his insistent tongue, and hers moved in return, tasting him, savouring the overt masculinity of the man. It was like a blissful dream—a dream where she knew she would soon wake, but for now. . .for now she would take each tender moment and cherish it for always.

Her hands moved as well, finding their way through the open front of his shirt. Webb's chest was muscular and hard, and the coarse hairs of his chest sent prickles of sensation through her finger tips. She felt Webb give a grunt of sheer animal pleasure as he felt her tender exploration, and then it was his turn—to unfasten the buttons of her blouse and let his tongue explore where his fingers were not enough.

The feeling was indescribable. Bonnie felt her nipples become taut with exquisite awareness and she arched herself up with a moan of delight. Craig had never made her feel like this. Never. . . Her body was on fire, and she was aching for this man to come closer. . .closer. . .

'Webb. . .' It was a pleading and a caress all in one and Webb pulled back, his eyes dark with passion.

'We're one, Bonnie Gaize,' he muttered savagely, his fingers entwining themselves in her soft brown curls. 'Deny it if you can.'

She couldn't. Not now.

This was a dream. Bonnie told herself the hard truth with something akin to desperation. How could she ever waken from this dream and face reality? How?

She couldn't—not when he was holding her as if she were the most precious thing he had ever beheld and the tenderness in his eyes melted her heart into a thousand shards of shimmering love. Webb. . .

His fingers touched the zip on the front of her jeans, and his deep eyes came up to question hers.

'Too soon, my Bonnie? I did promise you twenty minutes. . .'

A horn blasted right beneath them.

Bonnie jumped within Webb's arms, starting like a guilty child. What on earth. . .what on earth was she doing?

Their eyes met, the tenderness in Webb's suddenly replaced by laughter.

'The milk tanker. . .' he grinned. 'A blasted agricultural imperative. . .' The horn blared on, insistent and urgent. 'Have you filled in your chart, Bonnie Gaize?'

'I would have,' she whispered with an attempt at dignity. 'But. . .but I was distracted.'

'Sweet distraction. . .'

'Webb, I have to go!'

As one, they dived for the edge of the haystack. On the track below, the milk tanker had driven into the yard. Now the driver was standing beside the cab, one hand reaching into the truck to press the horn and the other held up to display his watch. Milk tankers ran to schedule and Bonnie was keeping this one waiting.

'Oh, help. . .' Bonnie's lips twitched and she turned to her love as he lay in the hay, peering down. He was covered in straw, his shirt was undone to the waist and his eyes were full of wicked laughter. 'I have to go down.'

'We'll both go,' Webb grinned. 'Hand in hand. Then you'll have to marry me.'

'Your reputation will be shot. . .'

'My reputation. . .' He turned and grasped her to

him. 'You're a one to talk of my reputation. You, who decided I was a philandering, double-crossing. . .toad, wasn't it? And now you worry about my reputation!'

'Webb, I have to go!' Bonnie writhed desperately out of his grasp and slithered over the edge. 'If I miss milk collection. . . Stay there!'

It was a desperate demand and she half-expected him to disobey, but Webb stayed where he was as Bonnie slid downward. Her hands fought to fasten her blouse buttons as she went and by the time she reached the bottom she was barefooted but almost respectable.

Now. . .

She took a deep breath, aware of the truck driver's amazed glance as she crossed the yard towards him, and fought desperately for a semblance of dignity.

'Good morning,' she called and her voice didn't sound the least bit normal.

The truck driver stared for a moment longer, and Bonnie knew she was covered in hay from head to foot.

'Chart's not filled in,' he said apologetically as though he'd realised he'd interrupted something of importance. 'Otherwise I could have picked up the milk and gone without. . .without disturbing you.' His lips twitched and the man dared to stifle a cough.

'I'm so sorry.' Bonnie was slightly breathless from the rush down—and from the exertion above—and she sounded like a guilty child. 'I was up in the haystack. . .setting. . .setting mousetraps.'

'Oh.'

She flashed him a suspicious look but the man had his face under control again and said nothing.

Bonnie filled in the chart with shaking fingers and then watched as the tanker driver emptied her vat, all the time aware that above them, looking down with unholy enjoyment, was Webb Halford. Her hay-strewn love. . .

Her bare toes tingled on the cold concrete of the dairy floor and she didn't care one bit. Cold toes were the least of her concerns.

Finally the tanker rumbled away, the driver giving her one last, long look as he went. Bonnie slumped onto a stone ledge at the dairy door. Moments later, Webb was beside her, shaking with laughter.

'My country bumpkin sweetheart. . .' He lifted a thatch of straw from her hair and kissed the place it had come from. 'It's not my reputation that's suffered now, Dr Gaize. It'll be all over the valley by nightfall that you were rolling in the hay with Dr Halford.'

'But he didn't see you. . .'

Webb grinned. He motioned across the yard to where his car stood, an elderly grey Bentley. 'There's not a lot of people in the valley who don't know the doctor's car,' he said simply. 'And if you think he believed for one minute that you were up in the haystack setting mousetraps—when firstly you hadn't finished the dairy chart which every good farmer does before he leaves the dairy, and secondly my car is here, and as a conscientious niece and doctor you should be in the house escorting the visiting doctor on his rounds. . .'

'Grace's car is there now, too,' Bonnie said desperately. 'He'll think you're inside with Grace.'

'I can see Grace and Paddy and Henry from the top of the haystack,' Webb told her. 'Grace has both men out on the veranda—in full sight of the tanker driver as he left. No sign of me—because I was up in the haystack otherwise occupied.' He pulled her up off the ledge and into his arms. 'So there's nothing for it, Dr Gaize. Your twenty minutes are up. Are you going to marry me, or will your name be broadcast as Kurrara's scarlet woman?'

'Webb, no. . .' Bonnie placed her hands against his

chest and held him back from her. Her eyes were troubled, regretting the dream already.

'What is it, my love?' He frowned. 'Sam? He's a good kid, Bonnie, and if you know how hungry he is for a permanent mum. . .'

Bonnie's face softened. 'Of course it's not Sam. He's a darling. But Webb. . .' She looked up at him, pleading for understanding. 'Webb, how can you know you want to marry me? It doesn't make sense.'

'Why ever not?' His voice held pure astonishment. He held her back from him at arm's length and his eyes went from the tip of her hay-strewn head to her bare, mud-squelched toes. 'How could I not fall in love with you, my disreputable, urchin love?'

'Love. . .' Bonnie shook her head, her eyes bright with unshed tears. 'It doesn't work, Webb. Not for me.'

'You mean because you were engaged once.' Webb's eyes darkened again. 'I can't but be grateful that he threw you over, but the man's a fool. . .'

'When you know me, though. . .' Bonnie took a deep breath, determined to make him see. 'It doesn't work. Even my parents didn't like me all that much——'

'What in heaven's name do you mean by that?'

His voice was so astounded that Bonnie stared. She shook her head.

'They didn't. Aunt Lois told me. . .'

'That woman. . .' Webb's hands pulled her savagely into him and he swore into her hair. 'Are you telling me there's no such thing as love because your parents didn't love you—when the only reason you're alive today is that they loved you too much to take you with them?'

'But. . .'

'I had a long talk with Grace Crammond about you,

Bonnie Gaize,' Webb said savagely. He swung her up again into his arms, ignoring absolutely her frantic protest. 'And about your ersthwhile aunt. It seems to me that you should have had the same talk ten years ago.'

'Talk. . .'

'Talk,' he told her. 'The only one in your family who ever talked was your aunt, and she seems to have instilled nothing but poison. It's time the poison was washed away.'

'Webb, please, put me down. . .' He was striding towards the house, his precious bundle in his arms, and Bonnie was helpless in his hold. 'You must. . . For heaven's sake, you must be needed at surgery. What if. . .what if someone's looking for you?'

'I left my mobile phone with Grace and she knows where I am,' he told her, ignoring her protests and keeping right on walking. 'Just as well, as things turned out. I don't think directing high pressured jets of water at mobile phones is recommended in the manual. The way you treat your menfolk, Dr Gaize. . .'

'You are not my "menfolk",' Bonnie told him with an attempt at dignity—no mean task when she was still barefoot, sodden and straw covered—and being carried in Webb's strong arms.

'Your menfolk have expanded by one,' Webb told her with ruthless tenderness. He smiled down at her with the smile that had her all undone. 'Maybe by two. Sam has no intention of being left out. So your menfolk are now Henry, Paddy, me and my Sam. Goodness, Dr Gaize, your horizons are expanding at every moment.'

'Webb, no!'

'Shut up, my love,' he told her kindly. 'Just shut up and listen.'

They were being watched. What Webb had told

Bonnie was true—Grace had brought Paddy and Henry out onto the veranda and they were watching the approach of the disreputable Bonnie and her bearer with varying levels of complacency. Grace looked like the cat who'd got the canary, but Paddy and Henry looked decidedly upset.

And so they ought, Bonnie thought desperately. She should be fighting this man tooth and nail—not lying back unresisting in his arms and trying not to let herself enjoy the sensation of being cherished.

Cherished. . . That was how this man made her feel. . .and Bonnie had never been cherished in her life. Not since her parents. . .

'Don't even think it, Bonnie Gaize,' Webb told her savagely, as he set her down on the big wicker settee on the veranda. How he had known her thoughts she couldn't tell, but that he had there was no question. 'Mrs Crammond?'

Grace's kindly eyes were beaming with curiosity and delight. 'Yes, Dr Halford?'

'Have there been any calls?'

Grace grinned. 'None that you'll know about until you tell us what's going on.'

'Conniving woman.' He shook his head at her and turned to Henry. 'Henry, your niece has just declined my proposal of marriage, and I need your help to convince her otherwise.'

'Marriage. . .' Given a large group of people like this Henry would never usually speak but he did now. His voice was a disbelieving growl and Webb smiled down at his worried face.

'Henry, I understand you think I'm married to Serena. Serena's my sister. My wife died three years ago. Now, given that I'm an almost respectable widower, have you any objections to Bonnie marrying me?'

There was a long, long silence and then a sudden crow of delight from Paddy.

'A wedding. . . If that's not something to live for then I don't know what is. I'm damned if I mightn't try harder at this breathing caper after all.'

'You do that, Paddy,' Webb told him. 'For we won't be married without you.'

'But I haven't. . . You're going too fast. . .' Bonnie's voice was practically a wail. She felt about ten, with things rollercoasting out of control around her.

'I am.' Webb lifted her hand and held it firmly in his, and his eyes gave her a message that took her breath away. 'But it seems to me that you've wasted a lot of time already.' He turned back to Henry. 'Did you ever tell Bonnie exactly how her parents died?'

Henry shook his head, confused and disoriented. 'Her aunt did at the time. . . The kid was so upset. . . Her aunt told me to keep out of it—that it was women's work. . .'

'So tell me what your aunt told you, Bonnie?' Webb demanded and Bonnie looked up at him with eyes that were as confused as her uncle's.

'They. . .they went to Italy on a holiday,' she whispered. 'They were speeding on a motorway and they crashed. They were killed outright.'

There were simultaneous gasps from both Henry and Grace.

'Of all the wickedness,' Grace exploded. 'If that woman was here now. . . I know you shouldn't speak ill of the dead—but that woman wants horsewhipping.'

'Tell Bonnie what you told me two days ago,' Webb interjected and Grace's angry flush died away. She looked down at Bonnie, her eyes bright with compassion.

'I never dreamed your aunt could be so vindictive,' she told Bonnie. She flashed an understanding look across at Henry. 'And at a guess, neither did your uncle, because I'm willing to swear he would never have agreed to telling you that. You know your father was a medical scientist, Bonnie?'

'Yes. . .' Bonnie winced. 'That's. . .I guess that's one of the reasons I went into medicine.'

'He was engaged on important research. There was a big fuss at the time about Thalidomide—you know—drugs causing birth defects. Well, your father was involved in testing series of lesser known drugs and I gather what he found had international repercussions. Anyway, his work had to be presented internationally to ensure the drugs would be withdrawn worldwide. There were two conferences he had to attend—one in India and one in Italy. There had just been an outbreak of plague in Bombay and there was no way your parents could take you there, so they had to leave you home.'

'So they left me here.' Bonnie's words were a painful whisper.

'Your mother didn't want to leave you,' Grace told her. 'She came to me just before she left and she was breaking her heart over it. She loathed Lois and she knew she'd give you a hard time. I offered to have you but I'd just had the twins and your mum knew it was impossible.' She took a deep breath. 'And she had to go.'

'Why. . . Why did she have to go?' Bonnie asked and it was Henry who answered her.

'Because your dad had a dicky heart,' Henry said savagely, his face tight with anger and his fists clenched hard down on the bedclothes. 'He had rheumatic fever as a kid and he was never strong. Your mum worried and worried—justifiably, as it turned out. The police reckon it was a heart attack that killed them both. Your dad was driving back to the hotel after the conference in Italy and he must have had a massive heart attack. He drove off the road into a post. He was dead at the wheel, with never a mark on him, but your mum was thrown out into the path of an oncoming car.' Henry's eyes filled with sudden tears. 'Dear God, Bonnie, I'm so sorry. Your aunt resented your mother—my sister—from the time I introduced them. She seemed jealous, of all things, and no amount of reassurance made a difference. She hated the fact that your dad was a doctor and they had more money than we did. But if I'd dreamed. . . If I'd known. . .'

'Then you might have found the courage to stand up to your wife?' Webb said softly. 'I wonder.'

He knelt down, then, and took Bonnie's hand in his. 'I'll leave you now, my love,' he told her gently. 'I've patients waiting. But believe that you are loved. First by your parents, and next, I suspect, by the two conniving old men in the beds behind me—and now by me. Very, very much.'

Bonnie could say nothing. She stared speechlessly at him, her white face shocked and wondering.

'I'll be back for Christmas,' he told her and stood. 'I told Serena last night where the wind lay—and she thinks we should all have Christmas together.'

'Together. . .' She fought for words. 'But. . . But Henry can't move. . .'

'Here,' he smiled down at her. He turned to Grace and smiled. 'What do you reckon? Should we have Christmas here?'

Grace was watching the conflicting emotions sweeping over Bonnie's face, and doubt was showing clearly in Grace's eyes. It hardly needed a mind reader to see what she was thinking—that this was right but Bonnie needed time to get her breath back.

'I've a suggestion,' Grace smiled. 'The rest of our family aren't due until tomorrow night and Neil's upset because we don't need our turkey—so how about we have a really big party here tomorrow? I'll bring Pete and Neil and the biggest turkey you've ever seen in your life. And a pudding. . . Goodness, do I have a pudding. It's the mother and father of all puddings!'

'And Serena knows a man whose mate's brother-in-law catches the best lobster in Australia,' Webb grinned. He spread his hands. 'Don't tell me where she finds all these contacts but if you want to find sea-fresh lobster a hundred miles inland, Serena's your woman.'

'And the grocer's coming this afternoon, isn't he, Bonnie?' Paddy asked anxiously. He coughed once and then repressed it firmly. Excitement tinged his pale cheeks pink. 'Blowed if I'll splurge on a bottle of whisky.' He grinned across at Bonnie. 'And a bottle of champagne. . . Or six!'

Despite her confusion and shock, Bonnie started to laugh. Their excitement was infectious, and so was their eagerness. They were all watching her now, willing her to approve, and she had never felt so surrounded by love in her life.

There was warmth in a heart that had been cold too long—love, like a rose bud, was slowly unfurling. It was still afraid of the wind and the elements, but bloom it would, whether she willed it or not. And Paddy and Henry. . . The transformation of her two gloomy patients was almost complete.

'I'll have to do some shopping myself, then,' she whispered. 'We haven't nearly enough bonbons.'

'That's my girl.' Webb pulled her to her feet and roughly into his arms. 'My Bonnie.' He bent and kissed her full on the lips, in front of them all.

'I know Grace doesn't want you bulldozed,' he said as he finally released her, smiling over at the smug-faced Grace Crammond. 'But there's no bulldozing to be done, my Bonnie. I've been knocked over since the first time I saw you. But now. . .I really do have to go.'

He turned then, but paused, staring down the drive. 'Are you people in the market for visitors? I think we have company.'

Then he whistled soundlessly as he saw who the visitor was.

'Good grief!'

## CHAPTER NINE

Now what? Bonnie took a deep breath, her fingers straying to bruised lips, and stared out where Webb was looking.

Unnoticed, a taxi had approached the house, halting by the house yard gate. Now a young woman with long black hair and tight, tight trousers was slamming the taxi door and turning to the group on the veranda.

'Jacinta. . .'

The woman was unmistakable. Bonnie hadn't seen her for four years, but she would have known her anywhere.

'Surprise, surprise.' Henry's daughter still had the same sulky voice Bonnie remembered so well. She stalked up the veranda steps and cold eyes swept over the group. They rested briefly on her bedridden father and then moved on.

'I don't know who the heck your friends are, Bonnie dear,' Jacinta continued silkily. 'But I think it's time you all took yourselves out of my house. Now!'

There was dead silence on the veranda. No one moved. All eyes were on Jacinta.

The woman deserved their attention. Jacinta's thigh-length hair was dyed a deep blue-black, too much make-up embellished a pixie-like face and her huge blue eyes were ringed with lashes that must surely be false. Her blouse was blatantly see-through, the black leather of her trousers clung to her like a second skin, and her glittering sandals had never been near the likes of a cow pat in their lives.

'Henry's other daughter, I presume,' Webb said at

last, and there was, amazingly, a trace of laughter in his voice. He held out his hand in greeting. 'I'm Webb Halford, your father's doctor.'

For the first time Jacinta's face softened as Jacinta took note of Webb's overt masculinity. The extraordinary lashes fluttered. 'Dr Halford. . . Well, of course I didn't mean you. I guess if my father needs medical attention then you can stay.'

'You mean you're not asking your father to leave?' Webb looked at the girl consideringly, his dark eyes raking her from the top of her gleaming head to the tip of her painted toe-nails. 'That's good of you.'

She flushed then, and pouted. 'Well, of course he can stay. He is supposedly my father, even if this is *my* farm.' She sighed and spread her hands. 'The rest though. . . I've a girlfriend who lives nearby and Susan rang to tell me what was going on. Such gossip. . . So I thought I'd pay my annual Christmas visit and clear up a few misconceptions.'

'Misconceptions?' It was only Webb doing the talking. Bonnie, the two men and Grace stayed silent, mesmerised by the ice in Jacinta's voice.

'You have no right to be here, Bonnie Gaize.' Again Jacinta turned to her cousin, and the ice in her voice grew colder. 'I thought we'd seen the last of you, but you have to come crawling back. . .'

'She didn't crawl. Your father needed Bonnie—or you.' Webb's voice was a douche of cold water but Jacinta didn't flinch.

'My father doesn't need her. None of our family needs Bonnie, or wants her either for that matter. We never did, and we never will.'

Somehow Bonnie made herself turn to Henry. His face was shocking. The colour had drained completely—and the laughter seemed as if it had gone forever. This was the haunted, hunted man Lois had terrorised through thirty long years of marriage.

Webb too was looking at Henry and what he saw made his eyes narrow.

'So now you're offering to come home to look after your father?' he asked Jacinta, his eyes still on Henry.

'If my father can't manage, then the farm has to be sold.' Jacinta's voice was clipped and cold, as though recounting a decision made long since. 'He'll have to move into a nursing home.' She turned once again to Bonnie and her eyes glittered. 'I thought he would have seen sense by now. He would have if you hadn't come back—butting in again where you're least wanted.'

'You told Webb. . .Dr Halford. . .he should contact me,' Bonnie stammered.

'Yeah, but I never thought you were stupid enough to come back. It's only since Susan rang and told me you were here that I figured what you'd want. You think my father has the power to leave the farm to you. He hasn't, Bonnie Gaize. It was my mother's farm and she left it to me—absolutely. My father can stay on it until he's dead or disabled—and then it's mine.'

'Lucky you.'

Once again Webb deflected Jacinta's attention. She turned, her eyes drawn to this dark, enigmatic doctor. Jacinta hesitated, obviously torn between malice and her desire to impress one drop-dead gorgeous male.

'Are you intending to nurse your father here?' Webb asked and Jacinta shrugged.

'He'll have to go into a nursing home. It's obvious. If he's still in bed after all this time. . .'

'Bonnie's been doing the milking and caring for the farm while your father recovers. Will you?'

Jacinta gave a hollow laugh. 'You have to be kidding! I'm not milking any cows.'

'My husband and son won't milk for you, Jacinta,' Grace Crammond broke in. 'And the farm will go bust if the cows are dry.'

'I couldn't give a stuff,' Jacinta said crudely. 'I told you—the farm has to be sold and if I lose because the cows are dry then I can cope with the loss. The land here should bring over three thousand an acre, and the sooner I have it the better.' She turned to Bonnie again. 'Now get your appendages out of here before I call the police and have you dragged off.' She pointed to Paddy. 'My farm is hardly the place for you to be playing doctors and nurses——'

'You little. . .' It was Paddy, propped up on his elbow, his normally pale face rapidly turning purple. He turned to Henry. 'Are you going to let your kid talk to you like that?'

'How do you think he'll stop me?' Jacinta spat. 'He knows I own this place and he's just a tenant. Tell them, Father dear. Tell them that you have no right to have anyone here—unless I say so.'

'She's right. It's her farm,' Henry said dully. He shook his head in weary defeat, but there was the beginnings of resignation behind his eyes. 'I've loved it. All my life I've loved it, but it's never belonged to me. So now. . .' Again he shook his head. 'I've been someone I don't like for most of my adult life because of how I felt about this farm. Now. . .the last week I've realised just how much this land has cost me, and it's time I stopped paying. Maybe if I have to get off the place then the sooner I go the better.' He looked directly at Jacinta. 'So you can order who you like off your farm—but I'll have nothing to do with it, and for the record, your behaviour disgusts me. So——' he looked up at Webb, his eyes pleading '—this nursing home you know. . . Can you get me in there?'

'Not yet, I can't.' Webb's eyes glittered with an anger

Bonnie hadn't seen since the first time she'd met him. He kept it in check however and his voice, when he spoke, was remarkably cool. 'If you or Jacinta no longer allow Paddy to stay here then his case is more urgent, but I think I can manage one place for Paddy. . .' He cast appraising eyes at the flushed Irishman, knowing Paddy's anger was a danger. If he let it explode it could cause a crisis with his breathing. 'I'll take Paddy into town with me now, if he agrees, and we'll collect his gear later. Henry, though——' Webb's lips tightened '—it'll be a few days before we can get Henry in anywhere. Meanwhile—— Can you cope with bedpans?' he asked Jacinta.

'Bedpans?' Jacinta's eyes widened. 'You're joking. He doesn't need bedpans any more.'

'He certainly does. Your father needs another week of total rest. His pelvis can't bear weight. Until that time he needs turning every couple of hours—more often during the day. He needs bed baths, massage and toileting. Are you prepared to do that?'

'Of course I'm not. He'll have to go to hospital.'

'There's no room for him in the hospital,' Webb told her bluntly. 'I refuse to acknowledge Henry's need as urgent when he has a legal right to stay here—and he has a right to have a nurse with him. Any legal adviser would uphold that right. That means if you won't nurse him, then he needs Mrs Crammond or Bonnie. . .'

Jacinta's eyes narrowed, and then turned appraisingly to Grace Crammond. Jacinta's overpainted mouth twisted into a semblance of a smile.

'Well. . .maybe I've been a bit hard. I'd forgotten you were once a nurse, Mrs Crammond.'

'It seems to me there's a few things you've forgotten—or never learned in the first place.' Grace Crammond was shoving her belongings into her handbag with fury. 'If you think you can put these people out on the streets and have me help you. . . Well, you've got another think coming, Jacinta Gaize.' She crossed to Bonnie and gave her a swift hug. 'You come to us if you need a bed tonight, dear. There'll always be a welcome for you with us.'

She'd said enough. Her face was the colour of Paddy's. She stomped down the veranda steps, climbed into her battered truck and roared off down the track.

'I have to go too,' Webb told them as the ancient roar of the truck receded. He looked briefly at his watch, clearly anxious to be rid of the whole affair. 'I'm an hour late for surgery already. Paddy, will you come with me?'

'Seems like I have no choice.' The Irishman threw back his bedcovers and put shaky feet into his slippers. He accepted Webb's supporting arm with gracious dignity, taking his cue from Webb, but as he was ushered past Henry's bed he stopped. The glare he cast Henry was more powerful than any words. 'Of all the weak-kneed, lily-livered. . .' His voice broke on a cough and Webb motioned him forward.

'Bring the oxygen, Bonnie. We'll go now.'

'I'm damned if Bonnie's staying.' Jacinta had her hands on her hips and glared almost as furiously as Paddy.

'Then you empty bedpans or wash sheets,' Webb said, with detached interest. 'Make up your own mind.'

He didn't speak again, but quietly ushered Paddy down into his waiting car.

Bonnie, after one look at her cousin's bitter face, followed them silently with the oxygen cylinder. Every nerve in her body was screaming to leave as well—to get out of range of Jacinta's vicious, cutting tongue. She couldn't leave Henry though. . . She couldn't.

Webb might believe Jacinta would be forced to do the right thing—but Jacinta was just as likely to let Henry suffer in bed, untended.

Webb hardly spoke as he put Paddy into the car. From where they stood, every word could be heard from the veranda, and Jacinta was listening as hard as she possibly could.

'Are you just going to drive off and let that tart do what she likes?' Paddy demanded as Webb closed the door on him.

Webb looked silently down into Bonnie's drawn face, and his mouth tightened. Briefly he raised a hand and brushed her face with his finger.

'I'll fix it,' he said softly. 'Trust me.'

The rest of the morning passed in a miserable blur. Henry didn't speak. He lay in passive silence as Bonnie ministered to his needs and tried to work out what on earth she was going to do.

Should she put Henry in a nursing home as Jacinta had demanded? Should she go back to Melbourne?

If only Henry would put up a fight for himself then she could help him. He had the right to stay here until he died—so he must be able to insist she stay as well.

It wouldn't work though, she realised, not if Jacinta had the right to stay as well; and her nasty tongue made every moment bitter. Jacinta and Lois had driven Bonnie out four years ago while Henry had passively watched, and now it was happening all over again.

'You needn't think I intend to be civil to you,' Jacinta snapped as the three were left alone. 'I'll put up with you because I have to, but the sooner we're shot of you——'

'Bonnie's been good to me, Jacinta,' Henry said wearily. 'She deserves better than this.'

'She's been good to you because she was suffering from delusions.' Jacinta had hauled her suitcases onto the veranda and paid off her taxi, making it clear that she was here to stay. 'This farm's valuable. I thought when you broke your pelvis you'd finally see sense and let me sell—but the same accident has obviously made Miss Goody Two Shoes decide you're worth being nice to. Nice for her if you could leave her something.'

'That's not the reason I came.' Bonnie's voice was a thread.

'Bonnie doesn't need our money,' Henry said sullenly. 'She's a doctor—and a good one, Jacinta. Plus Doc Halford wants to marry her—so her future's secure no matter what you manage to do to her.'

'Marry. . .' Jacinta's eyes snapped wide. 'Marry! Webb Halford—marry Bonnie? That's a joke.'

'I don't have to listen to this.' Bonnie clenched her fingernails into her palms. She took a deep breath. 'I need to clean out the milk vat. . .'

'Like a good little drudge,' Jacinta sneered. 'Keep the farm running in case of miracles. You always were a fine drudge, Bonnie Gaize, and now it seems Webb Halford knows a good thing when he sees one.'

'What. . .what do you mean by that?'

Jacinta laughed. 'You don't think a man like that would want you for your body, for heaven's sake? Susan told me the old doctor's dead and Webb Halford is desperate to find another—plus someone to look after his kid when his sister takes off overseas. He must be desperate if he wants you—but then, I guess the combination of drudge and doctor is too good to pass up.'

Bonnie's chin tilted. 'Webb loves me.' It was the first time she had acknowledged it even to herself, but the words had a thin ring to them—a hollow feel.

'Yeah? Like Craig did?'

'You should shut up about Craig,' Henry whispered

to his daughter. 'If you don't have a guilty conscience over that. . .'

'Why the hell should I have a guilty conscience? He was an attractive man and I went to bed with him.'

'He was engaged to Bonnie.'

'Well, that's hardly likely to stop any man from sleeping with someone else, is it now?' Jacinta smirked.

'I should have kicked him out.' Henry's voice was weary to the point of death and Bonnie's anger was replaced by a surge of concern.

'Kick Craig out?' Jacinta's laugh held nothing but scorn. 'Just because Bonnie wanted him gone. . . Since when have you had the right—or the guts for that matter—to kick anyone out of this place? This was my mother's farm, and you know it.' She picked up her suitcases from the veranda steps. 'You make me sick,' she said bitterly. 'The pair of you. God knows why my mother stayed married to you for so long. . .'

She slammed off into the house.

There was a long, long silence. Henry lay with his eyes bleakly on the veranda roof, staring at nothing.

The milk vat had to be cleaned. She should go, Bonnie thought bleakly, but she couldn't. Gently, she drew the bedcovers back, turning Henry skilfully in the bed to massage the tension-knotted muscles of his back.

He lay rigid, his muscles tight with pain and humiliation. Bonnie said nothing, just let her fingers do the work for her. After a while she knew that he was crying, tears silently slipping into the pillow under his face.

'Why did you stay married to Aunt Lois?' Bonnie asked after a while. She kneaded the small of his back, her fingers working over and over as they eased the tight, hard muscles.

A tremor swept over Henry and the tears checked.

For a while Bonnie thought he wouldn't answer, and when he finally did the words came from a long, long way away.

'I've never told anyone.'

'You don't have to tell me.' Bonnie let her fingers rest for a moment in a gesture of reassurance. 'It's just. . .it never seemed to me that you loved each other.'

'Love. . .' He gave a bitter laugh. 'Love! That's a joke.'

'You must have loved once,' Bonnie said gently. 'To have Jacinta. . .'

'Jacinta's not mine.'

The shock of the words passed through her. Bonnie could feel her fingers stiffen. With an effort she forced them to relax—to keep on with their gentle rubbing.

'Not yours? Does. . .does Jacinta know?'

'Of course she knows,' Henry said wearily. 'You don't think Lois would lose that opportunity to hurt me? That's why Jacinta calls me "Father", as if she's mocking me every time she says it.'

'Well, why. . .?'

'Because I was a fool.' Henry clenched his hands into the pillow. His voice was muffled, but clear for all that. 'I worked for Lois' dad as a kid—and I fell in love with the place. A farm had always been my dream, but my family—your mum's family—was churchmouse poor. So. . . So when Lois announced she wanted to marry me I was fool enough not to look too close at the reasons. I couldn't believe my luck. Lois was beautiful and strong-willed and she stood to inherit this place. . . And she was pregnant. Three months gone to another man. She told me on our wedding night.'

'Oh, Henry. . .'

'Lois always made it clear if I ever walked out

she'd tell everyone the baby wasn't mine—make me a laughing stock. . . And I didn't know until she died that she'd told Jacinta. Like a damned fool, I thought. . .I thought I ought to keep the knowledge from Jacinta. God help me, she felt like mine, even if she wasn't.'

There was nothing to say. Bonnie's agile fingers soothed and soothed. Her pity for this weak, biddable man knew no bounds. Sure he lacked spine—but he hadn't deserved Lois either.

'It wouldn't matter who found out now,' she said finally. 'No one's interested in what happened so long in the past.'

'Yeah, well it seems I'm finally doing what I should have done thirty years ago,' Henry said grimly. 'I'm finally leaving. It's the right thing to do—even if it chokes me to do it.'

So that was that. Henry would walk—or be carried—off the farm without a fight and Bonnie. . . well, things had happened too fast with Webb to be sure. She tried to drag back the happiness of an hour ago but it had dissipated into the morning mist. She worked through the morning in bitter silence, thankful only that there was so much to do that she had little time to think.

'He must be desperate if he wants you.'

Jacinta's words rang over and over in her ears. The old doubts were still there, with all there accompanying pain. Webb needed another doctor in the town, and he needed a mother for his son—and Bonnie was at hand as a solution to his problems.

It had to be that.

How could she possibly believe a man like Webb Halford could fall in love with someone like Bonnie? It didn't make sense. Bonnie's thoughts were almost unbearable, and when she finally heard a car travelling along the track it was all she could do not to run like a child out to meet it.

It wasn't Webb's. The woman emerging from the car was the nurse who had come to the farm the night of the crash.

'Doc Halford needs you in town,' the nurse told Bonnie bluntly as Bonnie and Jacinta appeared from different ends of the veranda.

'So you'll stay here now instead of Bonnie?' Jacinta's voice was hopeful and the woman shook her head. There was no smile. Whatever Webb had told her, clearly she saw no need to waste civilities on Jacinta.

'I'm here for just three hours,' she told them. 'Dr Gaize is to look after the surgery because Doc Halford has business to attend to.' She caught herself then, obviously remembering orders. 'He said, "If you wouldn't mind, could you please come, Dr Gaize?".'

'What. . .what sort of business?'

'He didn't say.' The woman set her lips as though she thoroughly disapproved of what was happening, and Bonnie wondered fleetingly just what it was she disapproved of. 'He just said he needed you.'

'Well, go on then,' Jacinta said nastily, hope replaced by disdain. 'If lover boy calls, then you'd better obey, Bonnie dear. It wouldn't do for our good doctor to think his fiancée has a mind of her own.'

Bonnie flushed, but bit her tongue on what she desperately wanted to say. Instead she collected her car keys and turned her back on her hateful cousin.

'That's never your car?' Bonnie's sports car was parked under a gum tree at the edge of the yard and Jacinta mustn't have noticed it before. Now her eyes widened in amazement. 'You're kidding. People like you don't have cars like that.'

'People like me shouldn't have cousins like you,'

Bonnie said grimly and ran the remaining few yards to her means of freedom.

Webb wasn't waiting for her. Instead there was a room full of patients and a curt note.

> Bonnie, I'm running hours behind after this morning and now I have an urgent appointment. Do your best with this lot. X.

As a love letter it left a lot to be desired. Bonnie stared down at the curt missive and hung on to the X at the end. He hadn't had to put it down.

The X was payment for obeying. He'd do the right thing by her if she did her duty—played the drudge.

The thought left her cold. Jacinta's words rang over and over in her ears as Bonnie settled down and saw one patient after another.

Somehow she managed to concentrate, blocking out unhappiness. There was the usual mix of afternoon surgery patients, and if she didn't concentrate she could miss something important.

'I'm glad you're thinking of staying, Dr Gaize,' her first patient told her. 'It's a darned shame your cousin came back though. You and Doc Halford could have lived at the farm. . .'

The whole town seemed to know of the morning's events, thanks to Grace Crammond and the milk tanker driver. Bonnie blushed and blushed again, and swore under her breath at the absent Webb. He was subjecting her to ordeal by fire and what business did he have on Christmas Eve that couldn't wait?

Christmas. . .

It was looking bleaker by the minute.

Ten patients. . . Fifteen. . . They went through in a steady stream, and Bonnie realised that for most of them, speed was of the essence. They wanted their health attended to fast because tomorrow was Christmas.

Finally there was one last patient to see. He was an elderly man, wizened and shaky with yellowed, jaundiced skin. He came unsteadily into her room, assisted by his palpably worried wife. As he lowered himself into a chair Bonnie could hear why he had come. The man was hiccuping steadily every few breaths.

'I can't make them stop,' he whispered desperately. 'I've had the damned things since last night and I've tried everything—cold keys down my back—drinking a glass of water backward—dry bread. . .'

Bonnie nodded, studying the man's history. Les Eeles had cirrhosis of the liver. By the look of his skin his condition was well advanced, with his liver hopelessly damaged. Hiccuping was one of the least deadly side effects of cirrhosis—but while hiccups lasted Les's life would be miserable.

There were drugs Bonnie could use—chlorpromazine, baclofen, nifedipine or even some of the strong anti-epileptic drugs. All of them had side effects which were capable of spoiling Christmas for Les, and maybe this was the last Christmas Les would spend with his family. His wife was ready to take him home. She wanted him awake and cheerful—not doped and withdrawn.

'The few treatments you've used are all granny remedies.' Bonnie smiled at the worried man before her, her mind considering and disregarding options with speed. 'They're often effective because they either directly or indirectly involve pharyngeal stimulation—the soft palate nerves in the throat cavity behind your mouth. So what I'd like to try is more of the same. I'll stimulate the nerves in your soft palate and see if we can stop the hiccups that way.'

'You mean. . .you won't just give me a pill?'

'A pill often isn't the most effective solution,' Bonnie assured him. 'And the ones that are generally useful may well make you sleep through Christmas.'

Bonnie's personal problems faded to the back of her mind as she struggled to reassure the man before her. Twenty-four hours of hiccuping had left him tired and frightened, and Bonnie guessed there was more fear within him than he was letting on. For the first time, this man's illness had taken his body out of his control—and it was a frightening feeling. She smiled her most reassuring smile. 'So I'd like to play with the back of your mouth—if you'll let me.'

'Will it hurt?' his wife asked doubtfully and Bonnie shook her head.

'It will be uncomfortable though,' she confessed. 'I might even make you sick—like putting fingers down your throat. But I'll probably stop you hiccuping.'

She didn't at first. Bonnie inserted a cotton wool bud into the man's mouth and gently massaged the anterior soft palate for about a minute. Les tolerated it with stoical calm—which in itself made Bonnie think it mightn't be effective. She needed those nerves to react.

Les hiccuped again as the cotton bud was withdrawn—and then again.

'If at first I don't succeed,' Bonnie said cheerfully, 'Try, try. . .' She smiled down at him, forcing cheer into her voice. 'Can I "try, try again"?'

'Don't mind me.' Despite his discomfort, Les managed an answering grin. Bonnie's cheerful good humour was infectious, and her concern for his problem was obvious.

'OK.' Bonnie flashed a look at his wife. 'Mrs Eeles, what I'm about to try might make your husband sick. If you'd like to stay outside. . .'

'I'd like to stay here, if it's all the same to you,' the

woman said, and her hand came forward to grasp her husband's.

There was real trust here. For a fleeting second Bonnie felt a stab of pain and recognised it for what it was. It was pure jealousy. These two had something she wanted so badly. . .

But only with Webb.

Concentrate, Bonnie Gaize, she told herself harshly as she prepared the equipment she needed. You can't think about Webb. You can't!

She didn't completely rid herself of Webb's image, but her mind was firmly on the job as she carefully inserted a nasal catheter.

The insertion was tricky with a conscious patient and took her full concentration. Les gagged a couple of times as the catheter slid down to where Bonnie directed it—directly opposite the second cervical vertebra. Normally Bonnie would call a nurse to help, but Mrs Eeles held the kidney bowl with one hand and her husband's hand with the other. She was a woman of steel.

Once in position the catheter worked like a charm. Bonnie jerked the catheter to and fro several times. Les retched and retched again but Bonnie's jerking was inexorable. Finally, satisfied, she withdrew the catheter.

There was a long, long silence. Both Les and his wife were waiting for what almost seemed inevitable—the next hiccup. It didn't come.

'Blowed me if you haven't stopped them,' Les breathed, and his iron-willed wife burst into tears.

'Well done, Dr Gaize.'

Webb. . .

Bonnie started and turned like a guilty child. Webb Halford must have a cat's tread. Like the Cheshire cat, the man appeared at will. Because Les was her last patient Bonnie had left the door open to the waiting room. Webb Halford was not leaning against the open door, his arms folded, surveying the messy little scene with appreciation.

'There aren't many doctors who'd go for the tricky solution rather than the pill bottle,' he told Les with a smile. 'You've been lucky with your choice of doctor.'

'I reckon it's you who's been lucky, Doc Halford,' Les Eeles whispered, still not brave enough to push his luck by raising his voice. He rose to unsteady feet and took his wife's arm. 'Thanks, lass. You've been a godsend.'

'The hiccups might return,' Bonnie warned, carefully averting her eyes from Webb. 'If they do. . .'

'Then we know where to find you,' Mrs Eeles smiled slyly, her eyes wholly on Webb. 'About six inches from Dr Halford I reckon.' She walked forward and planted a kiss on Bonnie's cheek. 'Thank you, my dear. Have a very happy Christmas—and the best of luck to both of you. I wish——' she broke off, and gave an expressive shrug '—well, I reckon the whole district will be wishing you well.'

She took her husband's arm again and they slowly walked out.

'So why aren't you looking at me, my Bonnie?'

As the Eeleses left the room Bonnie had retreated behind the desk and sat. Now she was staring down at her prescription pad as though her life depended on it.

'How's. . .how's Paddy?' she whispered.

'Seething.' Webb walked around behind her and took her shoulders in his hands. Gently he started to massage, working strong fingers into her skin. The sensation was indescribably good, yet it made Bonnie want to burst into tears.

'He's in the nursing home?'

'For the moment. He has a room to himself and a

view—but he needs to talk to you.'

'Then. . . Then I'll go now. . .'

With an effort, Bonnie shrugged Webb's hands away from her shoulders and rose. She turned but Webb was right there, blocking her path. He lifted her face with a hand under her chin, and studied her shadowed eyes.

'What's Jacinta been saying to you, my love?'

Bonnie sighed. 'You heard most of it. More of the same.' She shook her head. 'Please, Webb. . .I have to see Paddy.'

'And I've a woman in second stage labour,' Webb confessed. 'She's due to deliver at any minute.' His free hand came around her waist and he pulled her in to him. 'Damn! There's no time to talk and we need to. Bonnie, I just ask. . .whatever happens over the next few hours, I want you to trust me. Promise?'

'What. . ..what's going to happen?'

'I don't know,' he confessed. 'But I'm trying my darnedest to set things up—and I need your trust. Bonnie, love. . .'

'Dr Halford. . .' The receptionist called from the outer room. 'They're looking for you in the labour ward.'

Webb swore into Bonnie's hair and pulled her tighter. 'Promise me?' he demanded. 'Bonnie. . .'

'I trust you,' Bonnie whispered, her heart wrenching within her. What else could she do but trust him? What difference did it make?

His mouth lowered abruptly onto hers and she was kissed hard and long. It was a kiss of a man claiming his own before going off into the world. Who knew what the world held? but Bonnie was his, no matter what the future held.

'He'll do the right thing by me,' Bonnie whispered desperately to herself as he strode off to deliver babies and go back to his mysterious 'business'. 'As long as I trust him and do what's expected. And maybe. . . maybe I'm a crazy, childish fool to do it.'

## CHAPTER TEN

PADDY was as comfortable as he could be, but it took half an hour to pacify him and promise that at least Bonnie would come and see him on Christmas Day. The thought of the next day made both of them cringe, and as Bonnie directed her little car back to the farm she couldn't decide who was the most despondent.

'Drat Jacinta,' she muttered, and yet in her heart she felt a vague stirring of pity for the girl. Lois hadn't had to tell her Henry wasn't her father. What possible good had it done? It had driven a wedge between Henry and Jacinta, and for the first time Bonnie realised why Jacinta hated her so much. Bonnie was a legitimate, wanted child, and she was blood kin to Henry. Jacinta was neither of those things.

So be nice to her, she decided as she turned into the farm gate in the gathering dusk. Maybe if I'm nice. . .

There was no chance. Jacinta was on the veranda, drumming her heels with impatience.

'The nurse had to go an hour ago,' she snapped. 'You were supposed to be home by five. Father wants to use the bedpan and I said he'd just have to wait for you—and the cows have put themselves in the dairy. I'm damned if I'm milking them so you'd better get your backside into gear, Bonnie dear.'

Nice. . . It was all Bonnie could do not to slap Jacinta's overpainted face. She bit her lip with almost painful resolution and ran.

The cows took ages. The milking usually started by four or five o'clock, and a starting time nearer seven meant their udders were overloaded and they were tense and skittish. Bonnie worked until nine without a break, hoping Jacinta would do something about Henry's dinner. Jacinta certainly didn't come near the dairy.

'I don't know why on earth I'm continuing to milk,' she told the last cow for the evening. 'If Jacinta's evicting Henry and selling the farm. . .'

She couldn't stop herself, though. Like Henry, Bonnie loved this place, and for the time she was allowed to stay she'd keep the farm working.

At last she hosed down the yard and made her way back to the house—to find Henry with his bed still on the veranda and no sign of Jacinta.

'She's gone,' Henry said uneasily as Bonnie approached. 'And Bonnie, she took your car.'

'My car. . .' Bonnie stared. 'What do you mean? Has she. . . Is she gone for good?'

'No.'

There was something Henry wasn't telling her. Something. . . There was anger and pain in her uncle's eyes.

'Then where's she gone?'

'Webb. . . Dr Halford telephoned just after you started milking,' Henry said heavily. 'He wanted Jacinta to meet him for dinner.'

It was like a blow in the pit of Bonnie's stomach. She felt the colour draining from her face.

Jacinta and Craig. . .

Jacinta and Webb. . .

'Doc Halford's different to Craig.' Henry's voice was almost pleading. He put his hand out to grasp hers. 'Bonnie, it's different. It has to be.'

It has to be. Of course it has to be. Bonnie slumped down into a wicker chair and stared out into the darkness.

'So Jacinta's taken my car to meet Webb.'

'I said she should take the farm car. She just laughed.'

She would. Would Jacinta drive off into the night in a battered sedan when she could be behind the wheel of a sparkling new sports car? Would Jacinta respect the possessions of others?

Would Jacinta keep her hands from the man Bonnie loved?

She'd seduce him if she could, Bonnie knew, remembering the malicious delight Jacinta displayed when Bonnie discovered Jacinta and Craig together.

Why in heaven was Webb inviting her for dinner—on Christmas Eve too, when he should be at home with his family? Why?

'Trust me,' he'd said just that afternoon. Bonnie clutched at the memory of his words and felt little comfort. Jacinta and Craig, between them, had destroyed her trust. The world was a place of betrayal, and love made little difference. Love was a bargaining tool to be used by the powerful. 'Love me and therefore do what I want.'

Dear heaven. . .

'Have you had anything to eat?' she asked Henry finally, dragging her thoughts back to the mundane, and he shook his head.

'I'm not hungry, girl.' He gripped his hands tight on his coverlet. 'What the heck's the girl playing at? If she hurts you again. . . Heck, Bonnie, I should have taken you out of here when your mother died. We would have been broke—but maybe we would have been happier. It would have been better if I'd had the strength to just cut all ties and go. Go. . .'

That's what she should do, Bonnie thought wearily. Just go. Leave here and leave Jacinta with her legal gains—and Webb too if Jacinta wanted him.

Somehow she kept herself functioning. Somehow she pushed Henry's bed back inside, bullied him into having soup and toast and settled him for the night.

Merry Christmas, she thought bleakly, as she put the television on to be met with a broadcast of Carols by Candlelight. There had been some bad Christmases in her life, but this one looked a winner.

Where on earth was Jacinta?

Ten o'clock came. Bonnie checked Henry, and switched off the Christmas tree lights. The nurse must have turned them on before she left and the gay decorations looked incongruous and sad. This was no Christmas Eve.

Eleven. . .

Jacinta had been gone for four hours. Time for two dinners.

Eleven-thirty. . .

The clock chimed twelve and, as if on cue, the stillness of the night was disturbed by the noise of an approaching car, coming fast. The dogs woke from sleep, the hair on their backs stiffening.

The road leading to the farm was winding, twisting around the lee of the valley. The night was so still the sound of the car could be heard from a long way off. It was Bonnie's car—she knew its distinctive sound—and it was being gunned far too fast along the bends.

Far too fast. . .

Bonnie found she was holding her breath, in her mind steering her car around each of the bends. She knew the road so well. . . The car was being driven murderously fast.

The car sounded as if it was outside the Crammonds' now, spinning around the hairpin bend at the base of the gully.

The car screeched into the next gear as the driver put a foot flat to the floor. There was a stretch of straight road now, where the car could accelerate and accelerate. . .

Until. . .

'Slow down. . .' Somehow Bonnie was on the veranda, screaming uselessly into the night. The dogs were beside her, whining with fear and inside the house Henry woke.

'What the. . .?'

They both knew this track. They both knew exactly what would happen seconds before it did.

The car slowed by not a fraction. The little car hit the last bend, there was a dreadful, night-splitting screech of brakes that went on and on. . .

And then a violent, echoing crash, cut off horribly, horribly short, leaving only the echoes of tearing metal wafting around the stillness of the valley night.

'It's Jacinta,' Henry stated flatly into the dark and struggled to rise.

'No!' Bonnie was beside him in a moment, holding him down. 'Henry, you can't get up. Your pelvis won't hold you.'

'It's Jacinta. She's killed herself.' Henry gave a gasping moan and fell back onto the pillows. 'Bonnie, you know it was your car she took. She should have been back. That was the sound of your car. . .' He caught himself, his eyes widening in horror. 'Dear God, maybe she's with Doc Halford. . .'

Bonnie stared, horror doubling.

'She wouldn't. . .'

'She would if she could, girl, and you know it!'

Bonnie stared blankly at her uncle, her mind racing. No. . .

It was still there, the sickening memory of an afternoon four years ago. . .

The five of them—Lois and Henry, Bonnie, Craig and Jacinta, had gone to a town fête—and Jacinta had left early with a headache, sweetly asking Craig to drive her home. Bonnie couldn't leave as she was acting as first aid officer.

They could have gone anywhere—but Jacinta had brought Craig home to her parents' bed where she was sure Bonnie would find them.

She would if she could. . .

'Not Webb. . . Maybe Jacinta, but not Webb. He wouldn't hurt me like that. . . Please. . .'

She was wasting time.

Bonnie fought for calm as she ran to the phone. Three zeros. . .

'Police, fire or ambulance?' the operator drawled. Marie Baun had run the Kurrara telephone exchange since Bonnie was a child, and it took a lot to stir her to excitement.

'Marie, I need the ambulance,' Bonnie snapped, and then stared out the window in horror. There was a faint glow in the distance, growing brighter. 'And. . . and there's a fire too. There's been a car crash. . .'

'Where?' Marie was wide awake now. 'Is that you, Bonnie?'

'Crammond's lane at the head of the valley.'

'How many hurt?'

'I don't know. Get Dr Halford. . .'

'Dr Halford is unavailable at the moment,' Marie told her. 'Actually, Bonnie, he's out somewhere with your cousin—but he's carrying his mobile. I'll have the ambulance there in minutes and I'll try to contact him.'

Bonnie slammed down the telephone before she finished speaking.

'He's out somewhere with your cousin,' Marie had said. Dear God, let him not be in the car. . .

'Take the farm car. The keys are on the mantelpiece,' Henry called as she grabbed an armful of blankets. 'Bonnie. . .'

'Yes?' Somehow Bonnie made herself hesitate.

'Girl, you go steady. If she's killed herself. . .I don't want you dead too.'

'I promise.' Bonnie paused for a fraction of a second to give his hand a fast squeeze, and then she was flying into the night, choking on her fear.

The Crammonds reached the car before her. Their farm was marginally closer, and by the time Bonnie pulled to a halt beside the wreck, Grace, Neil and Pete were staring at the fire in dread.

Bonnie's tiny, frivolous car was a ball of flame. It had spun out of control—the tyre marks in the gravel were at crazy angles—and it had flipped before bursting alight. Now there was nothing but fire. Pete was directing a fire extinguisher, but it was a useless, token effort.

'Bonnie. . .'

As Bonnie climbed from the farm car, Grace stared as if she were a ghost. She walked forward, put her arms around Bonnie and burst into tears.

'Bonnie, love, we thought it was you.'

'Is she. . .is anyone underneath?' Bonnie whispered and Neil Crammond shrugged. The farmer looked numb and sick.

'Who can tell? If anyone's still there. . . If they are, then they're dead by now. Bonnie, who is it?'

'It's Jacinta. . .' Bonnie whispered. 'And maybe. . . Maybe Webb. . .'

'Dear God. . .' They turned as one and stared into the blaze, willing themselves to see into the flames.

'If there were two bodies in there, then surely we'd see something.' Neil, the normally phlegmatic farmer, was having trouble controlling his voice. 'The top was down. Maybe. . .' He walked back to his truck and retrieved a couple of torches, handing one to Bonnie.

'Let's check. It's possible that someone was thrown clear.'

Please. . . Bonnie flicked on the switch.

'Please. . .please. . .' As if in answer to Bonnie's silent plea, her unspoken word trickled up from below the ridge. It was a harsh, frightened whisper, but it was the sound of someone very definitely alive. 'Please. . .help me. . .'

Jacinta was lying in a pathetic heap just out of the pool of light thrown by the fire. The impact had thrown her over the lip of the valley road and about three yards down. Bonnie's torch picked her up in the dark, and the next moment she was crouched beside her, feeling her all over in the blackness.

'Jacinta. . . It's Bonnie. . .'

'You. . .' There was a trace of vindictiveness in Jacinta's voice and, for once, Bonnie was pleased to hear it. Fatal injuries didn't usually leave room for hatred.

'Don't try to move, Jacinta.' Bonnie's hands were running lightly over Jacinta's body, searching for gushing blood and compound fractures. Jacinta's upper body appeared OK, and she was moving both head and hands, but as Bonnie's hands reached her leg the girl gave a stifled scream.

'What's wrong?' Neil Crammond was with them, his torch adding its glow to Bonnie's and then Grace appeared as well.

'You've broken your leg, Jacinta,' Bonnie told her cousin, fighting back her most urgent question. She couldn't ask it. She was scared to death of what she might hear.

Neil Crammond knew no such hesitation. 'Was there anyone else in the car?' The man had no compunction in questioning Jacinta through her pain. He wanted to know, and he wanted to know now. His question was brutally harsh, and Bonnie closed her eyes, preparing for agony.

Jacinta stared up at Neil, as though regretting the word she had to utter. Neil stared right back, defying her to lie.

'N-no.'

The relief at the word was indescribable. Bonnie sank back on the uneven ground, dizzy and faintly nauseous with relief.

Jacinta's face twisted and her voice filled with a mixture of pain and defiance. 'But I've crashed your car, Bonnie.'

'It doesn't matter,' Bonnie said gently. Relief was washing over her in waves. 'You'll be OK and that's all that matters. Things can be replaced. People can't.'

There was a deathly silence.

'You think that?' Jacinta quavered. 'Of me?'

'We'll talk later.' Bonnie pressed her firmly back against the grass. 'Just lie still.'

Jacinta whimpered and then began to sob. If only Bonnie had some morphine. . .

She cast a quick glance up at the flames. Bonnie kept a fully equipped doctor's bag with everything she needed in the luggage compartment of her little car. A fat lot of use it was there. It was now solidly part of the fire.

The distant scream of an ambulance siren came from nowhere, building until its crescendo split the night. Bonnie breathed easier as its siren cut on the road above. Jacinta's face was bloodless with shock and pain. Soon. . .

The vehicle pulled to a halt at the ridge. There was a shout and then Webb's silhouette appeared above against the glow from the dying flames.

From where they crouched over Jacinta they were

almost invisible from the road and Webb had eyes only for the crash.

'Bonnie. . . That's Bonnie's car. . . Dear God, Pete, tell me she's not in there. . .'

It was a hoarse shout of despair and it took Bonnie's breath away with the anguish behind the words.

The anguish was real. The anguish was for her.

There was a yell of reassurance and the silhouette turned. Webb stood stock-still, staring down at the torchlit figures below, and then he was moving downward, fast into the night.

The recumbent Jacinta, Grace and Neil were ignored. Bonnie was lifted, gathered to Webb as though she were the most precious thing in the world, lost and now found again.

The most beloved. . .

'I thought it was you. . . They just said there was a crash—and it was your car——'

Webb's voice was hoarse with passion and shock, and his tone stilled any doubts. 'Dear love. . .I thought it was you. . .I couldn't bear it. . .'

Bonnie put her face against his chest and let her tears flow. This was more than a declaration of love. This was the pain she had felt, and it was returned in full.

You are my everything. . .

Jacinta's leg was a simple tibial fracture—not a difficult task to reduce but it needed an anaesthetist as well as a surgeon.

It was almost surreal, to stand in the operating theatre beside Webb after the events of the day and make her mind concentrate on medicine.

Webb, at least, seemed clinical, switching into efficient surgical mode as he donned his gown and mask, and if his eyes twinkled warmly over the green linen it didn't affect the deftness of his fingers. It was only Bonnie whose colour refused to subside as she forced herself to concentrate on the anaesthetic.

'She was breaking the law by not wearing a seat belt,' Webb told Bonnie as he carefully pinned the broken bone. 'But if she hadn't she'd be dead.'

'She was breaking the law by travelling at the speed she was.' Bonnie looked down at the white, unconscious face of her cousin. 'Poor, silly girl. . . She has so little.'

'You can find it in you to be sorry for her?' Webb asked. He looked up at his anaesthetist and his eyes gently questioned over his mask.

'Yes.'

I can find it in me to be sorry for anyone who's not me, Bonnie thought hazily, as their eyes met. Her heart was doing crazy, silly jumps and her eyes smiled directly at her love.

'Stop looking at me like that, Bonnie Gaize,' Webb growled. 'I'm supposed to be concentrating.'

So was Bonnie. She turned back to her dials with a visible effort.

'Do you know why she was travelling so fast?' Webb asked after a while.

'No.' Bonnie shook her head and then a thought struck her. 'You saw her last. Do you?'

Webb glanced up at her, and then swiftly back to his work. His hands moved skilfully at what he was doing. The bone was in position and he was starting to adjust traction. Jacinta would suffer no lasting damage from this night's work.

'I told her she couldn't sell the farm.'

'I beg your pardon?'

It was so hard to concentrate with him so near, and yet she must! Bonnie was going to have to learn to work with this man while he looked at her like that.

Behind them, the theatre sister looked from Bonnie to Webb and back again, her eyes wide with unasked questions.

'I spent this afternoon with the local lawyer—and with Grace Crammond,' Webb told her, his eyes not leaving his work. 'They tell me your uncle has worked the farm for over thirty years. In that time he's never taken a holiday, although Lois took many. He also employed a housekeeper while Lois was alive because Lois didn't like housework. Therefore, in the lawyer's opinion, Lois didn't have the right to leave the farm only to Jacinta in her will. I told Jacinta so this evening. Reverse now please, Dr Gaize. . .'

Reverse. . . Mechanically Bonnie reversed the anaesthetic, her mind racing. Concentrate. . .

It wasn't until Jacinta was wheeled back to the ward, her breathing settled, that she found the strength to question.

'Then. . . Then Henry can stay?'

'For however long he likes, and with whoever he likes,' Webb told her. 'If he has to mortgage the farm to pay for nursing then there should be no problem. He needs to put in legal application to challenge Lois' will, but the challenge should be upheld.'

They were alone at the sink now, the rest of the staff settling back into normal duties. The theatre lights were dim. They stood, garbed in theatre green, two colleagues who had just performed a satisfactory piece of surgery. They should now calmly bid each other good night and go home.

Instead they stood, looking at each other like two parts of one whole. Bonnie couldn't meet Webb's eyes. She was watching a small smudge just about at Webb's breast, as if her life depended on it.

'We should go home,' Webb said softly, echoing Bonnie's thoughts.

'Henry's car is still at the crash,' Bonnie murmured. 'I'll. . .I'll have to get a taxi.'

'Our only local taxi driver is long ago in bed,' Webb told her, taking her firmly into his arms. 'Where all sensible people are at this hour of Christmas Eve—or Christmas morning rather. Sleeping soundly, dreaming of Santa Claus, sugar plums and too much plum pudding. No, my Bonnie. Grace is at the farm with Henry, and if I know Grace she's expecting to stay. You're coming home.'

'Home. . .'

'To my home, my heart,' he said softly, and lifted her face to be kissed. 'My heart, my home, my life.'

# CHAPTER ELEVEN

AS CHRISTMAS dinners went, it was magnificent.

Three tables dragged together on the farm's veranda were barely enough to bear the food. Between them, Grace and Serena had produced a feast for kings.

For Kings. . .

For Kings and Queens and Princes and Princesses. . . Champagne, lobster, turkey, cranberry sauce, garden fresh strawberries, home made ice-cream, a pudding so rich it was almost black, stuffed with figs and apricots and mango, and served with lashings of brandy butter and clotted cream straight from the dairy. . .

The Crammonds, Serena and Sam, Paddy and Henry. . . They were all there. All the people that Bonnie loved. And Webb. . .

Webb's son was snuggled between the pushed-together beds of Paddy and Henry. Sam's disgust at the fate of the Noddy car had been tempered by explanations of insurance-funded replacement. Now he slept off excitement and Christmas pudding, and Woofer, the brand new puppy on his chest, did likewise.

Webb had brought Paddy back to the farm that morning. Now Paddy was extolling the virtues of whisky, while Neil and Pete Crammond were placidly vocal in defence of beer.

In the bed beside Paddy, Henry just smiled and smiled. The yoke of oppression had lifted, and the removal of its weight would take some getting used to.

'As will those pyjamas.' Serena laughed down at the

two men in bed. 'Honestly, Bonnie. . . What woman in her right mind would buy red satin pyjamas emblazoned with hearts for these two degenerates?'

'Only my Bonnie,' Webb smiled. 'Only my Bonnie. . .'

Bonnie hardly heard. She sat on the veranda a little apart from the rest, Webb's arm holding her tight. The sun was on her face. The world was at peace and she was with her love.

'I've been thinking,' Webb murmured into her ear and she smiled.

'I haven't room left to think,' she whispered. 'I've had one—or maybe three—too many helpings of Christmas pudding. I'm sure it's the brandy butter that's making me light-headed.'

'Well, maybe it'd be more honest to say I did some thinking yesterday. So now I have something to tell you. . .'

'What?' She was hardly listening, drifting in a haze of happiness.

'I've offered Jacinta payment for the portion of the farm Henry will be obliged to bequeath her.'

Bonnie's heart stilled. 'And. . .and she accepted?'

'She didn't like it. She was furious to know she had no rights at all to the farm while Henry was alive and Henry still had some control over who he could leave it to when he died. That's why she stormed out and crashed the car. It was a generous offer, though, Bonnie. I gather Jacinta's in a tricky financial situation, and she's horrified to know Henry could live for twenty years. I've offered her enough to set herself up with a flat in Sydney, if that's what she wants, and she's accepted, waiving all rights to the farm. So now. . .'

'Now?'

'Now, I propose we build another house—in fact another two houses on this farm. It's only five minutes from town, so we can travel to work from here. Between the pair of them, Paddy and Henry can run the farm for a good while yet, and it's a great place for Sam to grow up. Serena—well, Serena wants her own studio and apartment, and she's already thinking of the best place to build a kiln out behind the dairy.'

'It sounds like a commune,' Bonnie smiled and Webb touched her nose.

'I had the idea when you lost your gumboots and I saw you in bare feet,' he grinned. 'All you need is flowers in your hair.' His smile deepened. 'But no, Bonnie. Not a commune. It's going to be a family farm—for all of us. And for you and me and Sam. . . We'll build the biggest house of all. . .'

'The biggest house. . .' Bonnie could only repeat his words, her heart near to bursting. 'For you and me and Sam. . .'

'And Woofer,' Webb smiled. 'And cat Christabelle and my fierce protector, terrapin Mabel.' He rose to his feet and pulled Bonnie with him. 'And for whoever else chances along—if they should just happen to arrive.'

'After last night you should be prepared for the worst,' Bonnie smiled, her heart turning somersaults. 'Oh, Webb. . .'

'And I've bought you a Christmas present, Bonnie Gaize.'

She stared up at him. 'But. . . Webb, I haven't bought you anything. I haven't. . .'

'You needn't buy me anything,' he told her, and he kissed her gently on the lips. The sounds of voices behind them faded to nothing. 'My lovely Bonnie, you need purchase nothing. You give the gift of giving. . . the gift of loving. You give me love, my Bonnie, and that's all I ask. It's all I'll ever ask of you.' He put his hand in his pocket and brought out a tiny, square container. 'But my gift is something more tangible—something for me as well as you.'

Bonnie looked down at the small, velvet box in his hand and her eyes filled with tears. 'Webb. . .'

He lifted the lid. Nestled on black velvet was a single, solitaire diamond, twinkling in the sun like a thousand stars.

Then, before Bonnie could lift it from its box, Webb's face changed as he caught a movement below the steps. He turned to look, and his deep, smiling eyes creased in delight.

'Another Christmas present!' he announced with joy, and the delight in his voice caught the attention of all on the veranda. 'Or more if I'm not mistaken. Five. . . Six. . . A whole brood of Christmas presents, Bonnie Gaize. . . Just for us.'

They were all awake now, the whisky-beer argument forgotten and sleepiness receding. Sam's puppy lifted his nose to utter a protesting whimper as Sam clambered over Paddy and off the bed.

'It's a chook, Dad,' the little boy shouted, squeezing in between Bonnie and Webb. 'It's a black and white chook with black and white chickens. . .'

'It's Frankie,' Henry hooted from his bed. 'Well, what do you know! She must have met up with her Johnnie and decided on a spot of domesticity.'

'Sounds good to me.' Webb was lifting the third finger of Bonnie's left hand and sliding the diamond home. 'Frankie and Johnnie and family.' His eyes devoured Bonnie as he spoke, and his unspoken message said nothing at all about chooks.

'Frankie and Johnnie. . .' Sam gave a small boy's crow of delight. 'They've had babies. Lots of them. I can count eight.'

'Hey,' Paddy chuckled. 'How about that? Frankie and Johnnie. . .and a Bonnie as well. . . All we need now is a Clyde to complete the set.'

A Clyde. . . Bonnie and Clyde.

'Will a Webb do?' Webb asked and he looked down at his love with the faintest trace of uncertainty in his eyes. His hand rested on his son's dark head but his eyes were all on Bonnie. 'Will a Webb do, my Bonnie?'

Bonnie looked straight back at him, her eyes bright with unshed tears.

'A Webb is a perfect match for a Bonnie any day,' she whispered softly. 'A Webb is my perfect Christmas blessing.'

# A year's supply of Mills & Boon Romances—absolutely FREE!

Would you like to win a year's supply of heartwarming and passionate romances? Well, you can and they're FREE! Simply complete the wordsearch puzzle below and send it to us by 30th June 1996. The first 5 correct entries picked after the closing date will win a years supply of Mills & Boon Romances (six books every month—worth over £100). What could be easier?

**READER SERVICE**
**ROMANCE**
**RESIST**
**HEART**
**MEMORIES**
**PAGES**
**KISS**
**SPINE**
**TEMPTATION**
**LOVE**
**COLLECTION**
**ROSES**
**PACK**
**PARCEL**
**TITLES**
**DREAMS**
**COUPLE**
**SPECIAL EDITION**
**EMOTION**
**DESIRE**
**SILHOUETTE**
**MOODS**
**PASSION**

| | M | E | R | O | W | A | L | R | L | M | S | P | C | O | S | | |
|---|---|---|---|---|---|---|---|---|---|---|---|---|---|---|---|---|---|
| | O | | E | C | I | V | R | E | S | R | E | D | A | E | R | | |
| R | O | | | | | | | E | | O | S | M | A | E | R | D | S |
| O | D | H | E | A | R | T | | S | | S | | S | E | L | T | I | T |
| M | S | | | | S | | E | | M | E | M | O | R | I | E | S | S |
| A | E | | | | C | G | | | | S | A | | C | | | | E |
| N | P | T | | | A | | | E | K | | W | | O | I | | | W |
| C | | | T | P | K | I | S | S | C | | | | L | T | T | | O |
| E | | | | E | | | H | | A | E | V | O | L | | E | N | N |
| | | A | E | | U | | M | | P | R | | T | E | I | M | O | E |
| | | E | N | | L | O | | | L | I | | S | C | | P | I | O |
| | S | L | I | | | | H | A | | S | | I | T | | T | S | A |
| | | P | P | A | R | C | E | L | N | E | | S | I | | A | S | Z |
| | | U | S | D | B | | | | I | D | | E | O | | T | A | I |
| | O | O | | O | | N | | | B | S | | R | N | | I | P | S |
| | | C | | E | N | N | A | M | T | R | R | L | G | N | O | L | T |
| | | O | | E | M | O | T | I | O | N | | | O | | N | | I |
| | N | O | I | T | I | D | E | L | A | I | C | E | P | S | K | | |

*Please turn over for details of how to enter...*

## How to enter

Hidden in the grid are words which relate to our books and romance. You'll find the list overleaf and they can be read backwards, forwards, up, down or diagonally. As you find each word, circle it or put a line through it.

When you have found all the words, don't forget to fill in your name and address in the space provided below and pop this page into an envelope (you don't need a stamp) and post it today. Hurry–competition ends 30th June 1996.

Mills & Boon Wordsearch
FREEPOST
Croydon
Surrey
CR9 3WZ

Are you a Reader Service Subscriber? Yes ❑ No ❑

Ms/Mrs/Miss/Mr ______________________________

Address ______________________________

______________________________

______________ Postcode ______________

One application per household.

You may be mailed with other offers from other reputable companies as a result of this application. If you would prefer not to receive such offers, please tick box. ❑

COMP295
F

DMA

mps MAILING PREFERENCE SERVICE